The Horror Collection
Pink Edition

Other Books by KJK Publishing

Collections

Dark Thoughts

Vampiro and Other Strange Tales of the Macabre

Anthologies

Collected Christmas Horror Shorts

Collected Easter Horror Shorts

Collected Halloween Horror Shorts

Collected Christmas Horror Shorts 2

The Horror Collection: Gold Edition

The Horror Collection: Black Edition

The Horror Collection: Purple Edition

The Horror Collection: White Edition

The Horror Collection: Silver Edition

100 Word Horrors

100 Word Horrors 2

100 Word Horrors 3

100 Word Horrors 4

Carnival of Horror

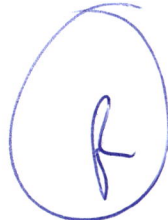

Novels and Novellas

Pandemonium by J.C. Michael

You Only Get One Shot by Kevin J. Kennedy & J.C. Michael

Screechers by Kevin J. Kennedy & Christina Bergling

Stitches by Kevin J. Kennedy & Steven Stacy

Foreword

Whether you are reading this book as a standalone or part of The Horror Collection series, I hope you enjoy it immensely. Each book has allowed me to work alongside authors who I love, and it lets me bring something new from them out into the world. The authors in these books are my own personal favourites. Some of them I have been following for years and others I have discovered more recently but, in each case, I have found a voice I need to keep reading. I hope you enjoy their stories as much as I did.

Kevin J. Kennedy
Editor

Acknowledgements

I'd like to thank Darren Tarditi, Ann Keeran. Michael Bray, Tim Curran, Kyle M. Scott, Douglas Hackle, Mike Duke, Zoey Xolton & Natasha Sinclair. I'd also like to thank everyone who continues to support me on this amazing journey.

Kevin

Table of Contents

That Song I Love

By

Kyle M. Scott

Frank watched the rain cascade down the windowpane, running in determined little rivers toward the outer sill, where it sank into the corroded wood and seemed to warp it before his very eyes. A spider web stubbornly clung to the top left corner of the window, while the autumn wind did its very best to tear the intricately woven weave asunder. The spider, Frank noted, was nowhere to be found. He wondered if it had moved on to pastures new, finding this initial webbed homestead to have been positioned in an altogether too damn creepy location.

And who could blame it if it had?

If *he* could afford it, Frank would do the same thing and get the hell out of there for good and ever more.

Get the hell away from that view out there.

But he couldn't afford it. And unlike his missing arachnid friend, he couldn't pull another home out of his ass, no matter how wide his ass was growing. Chances were the eight-legged little transient had shuffled off this mortal coil anyway; probably frozen to death by these god damn October winds or eaten by a larger specimen of its own kind.

Did spiders feed on their own?

Maybe.

He could recall reading something about certain mating rituals in high school. Didn't some of the females of the species chow down on the males after they'd gotten boned? Yeah... he was sure of it.

Frank caught a glimpse of himself, reflected in the console's shiny black surface. He grimaced at the sight of the stranger looking back, bored, dead-eyed and sullen as a fucking teenager bathed in the overwrought meanderings of an Emo rock binge.

Christ, Frank. Look at you now; once a local legend for your wild ways... reduced to dwelling on the life, death, and practices of a fucking bug that you're starting to genuinely think has, or had, a better life than you do.

Pathetic.

Still, his choices *were* limited. It was either muse on a bug's life or pay attention to the droning, rambling

10

nonsense that the latest caller was babbling into his ear (via a headset that had cost an arm, a leg, and a weekend's worth of bourbon).

And that was no choice at all.

Not to mention, should he tune out both the caller's mind-numbing, nonsensical political diatribe *and* shift his focus from the tough little web and its absent creator, there was only one other thing he'd have to focus on, now that the drink was close to be being done and sobriety still clung to his mind and body like that fucking little spider web clung to the window...

The cemetery out there in the rain.

Frank had no intention of letting that damnable place get the better of him. He wasn't a superstitious man, but nighttime was nighttime, and the dead should be left in peace without some desperate disc jockey eyeballing their sodden plots in the dark of an autumn night. A man's abode wasn't supposed to overlook such places, and a man's mind (however fried by liquor and bitterness it may be) should never, *ever* run away with itself when in close vicinity to such a place. It was all too easy to imagine the coffins down there, buried deep within the soaking, cloying earth; their inhabitants staring with dead, eyeless sockets into forever. One plot in particular had been the unwelcome catalyst for his ever more frequent creep-outs, during these last few weeks. The fresh one, just beneath the ancient burr oak tree and within a stone's throw from where he sat.

He could still see the funeral for that one in his mind's eye.

And, when he let his mind get away from him, he could see the body down there too. Except in that grave, the occupant's eyes were not yet rotted. They stared not into forever but, instead, they searched for him.

Who needed that shit playing on their imagination at 2:45 in the morning? He rubbed his eyes and turned his attention to the sky out there. The harvest moon hung high, wreathed in dark clouds that occasionally eclipsed its hollow light. Thunder rumbled off in the distance, beyond the hills and valleys that bordered the town. And the rain kept on raining.

Summer felt a long way off.

"D'you get what I'm saying?" the guy on the other end of the line asked.

Nope. Missed every word, you boring fuck. "I hear you loud and clear, my friend," Frank replied in his best approximation of an interested party.

That was all it took for the man on the other end of the line to charge ahead with his rant, spitting venom over the airwaves about *this* senator or *that* congressman when all he was *required* to do was pick a goddamn song, dedicate it to someone, and shut the fuck up already.

Damn, he was tired.

This whole radio-host gig would be so much easier if he could hire a stand-in, just for one or two nights a week. But the right staff were even more costly than the microphones, their processors, the broadcasting software (and local license to use it), and the mountain of other overheads that he'd had to shell out for, to get this damn radio station on the air. His ex-girlfriend, Lynette, had been of little to no use either. She hadn't been worth the wages he hadn't paid her, and she was gone now anyway. Good riddance.

When it came right down to it, the taxman's knock on the door was never too far off. Bankruptcy hung like the sword of Damocles above his bed, held by slowly fraying rope that was fixing to snap at any moment.

Snap, plunge, thwack... fucked.

And what did all these expenditures and perilous financial conundrums lead to? Well, they led to a guy being forced to set up shop in the cheapest building in the area; in a place that's price betrayed its undesirability. The sort of place no one in their right mind wanted to live or work. Or (as was currently the case for Frank Simmons) both.

An apartment in the middle of nowhere overlooking a goddam boneyard, for instance.

The thunder drew nearer. Lightning lanced the heavens. Frank concentrated on the web and on the wind, and when he sensed the irate caller was beginning to wind down, *get to the fucking point, and pick your song*, mused Frank, he once again feigned interest. It was easy. Most people didn't give two shits whether you were listening to them or not; they just wanted to hear the sound of their own voice whilst they were on live radio, however small the station.

Look, Ma... top of the world!

Bunch of bullshit.

He'd gotten into this gig with dreams of an easy life; envisioning himself sat on his ass with a spliff in one hand and a bourbon in the other, while he rolled out tune after tune of timeless rock, blues, and soul music: The Doors, Leadbelly, Aretha Franklin, The Lovin' Spoonful, The Cramps, Simon & Garfunkel. The problem was that the dream had holes. Some small, some as big as a chasm. The bourbon had become a crutch, more a habit than a pleasure, that was a small hole. Worse were the callers' requests. The songs that they asked him to play were often those of the more mainstream variety.

In other words, the sort of shit he abhorred listening to.

Should have seen that coming. Popular songs were popular… go figure.

Throw into that mix the necessity of working nights (because *night time was the right time in Colorado Springs)* and a two-bit apartment sat atop a mausoleum, overlooking what had to be the creepiest boneyard outside of a classic Universal fright flick, and you had a dream that was rapidly turning into a nightmare.

Wasn't life a gas gas gas?

The guy on the other end of the line stopped talking about whatever he'd been talking about. Frank took a sip of the sour bourbon and closed his eyes as he spoke.

"That's some food for thought there, my brother. Food for thought, indeed. Now, what song would you like to hear and, if you're of the mind, who would you like to dedicate it to?" In the moment between his questions and man's answers, Frank silently cursed John Carpenter.

If you hadn't made DJing look so god damned enticing in *The Fog,* I wouldn't be in this shitshow situation, he rued.

"Oh, well thanks for asking," the caller replied. He sounded elderly. And well-mannered. That was a good sign.

The oldies loved the goldies after all.

Coming up... a stone-cold classic from the halcyon days of —

"I'd like to hear that new one by Beyonce."

Jesus. "You got it, buddy."

"She got a song out just now that is *so* catchy. They play it down the bingo hall a *lot*. Most of the ladies down there love it and it's gotten its claws into me, son. Now, what's its name...?"

Son of a bitch. Frank knew the song. Frank hated the song.

"Don't sweat it, my friend. I have it right here."

16

"And I'd like to dedicate it to my ex-wife, Gemma, if I may."

"Sure," he answered, doing his best to sound enthused. "This one's for you, Gemma. We hope you're listening, wherever you may be."

Probably as far away from this guy and his musical tastes as you can legally travel, Frank mused.

"And *I'll* be right back after this slice of modern pop, loyal listeners. Don't you go anywhere, now, you hear?"

Frank hit 'mute', lined up the song, and hit play. A few more cents in Beyonce's pockets.

He pulled the new and expensive headset off, dropped it on the desk, and rubbed his eyes. A headache was coming, sure as priests paid attention to schoolboys.

A thousand years and three minutes later, the song the old fella had chosen drew to its close, it's autotuned songstress's voice fading away in time with the overproduced synth score, until there was little left but the bliss of silence. Frank basked momentarily in the clean airwaves. He was close to drifting off. He punched the 'unmute' key, pulled on the headset and said, "That was Beyonce's latest, folks. Thanks for the call, friend. We'll be taking more calls in just a little bit, folks, but for now here's a song that's close to my own heart. This one's by Dion, and it's called 'Only You Know'. Enjoy..." he crooned in his best laid-back drawl. The layered melodies kicked in on Dion's lost recording and Frank sighed deeply, basking in the warm glow. Good music was like honey to the bee, and when a bee like Frank was deprived of its honey, it tended to sting indiscriminately. He had no intention of coming across as an asshole for the last hour of his show, and that was exactly what'd happen if he'd have to endure another 'song' selected by the public.

He let the music fill the concert hall between his ears. Just a taste. That would do. Just a taste. Then the next caller could pick a song and most likely make a strong case for why 'ideocracy' was no longer a concept but a full-blown fact of life.

Maybe he'd get lucky. Maybe the caller would have a predilection for the greats. Maybe not. Either way, the fucker on the line could wait a few more minutes until Dion's criminally overlooked classic had played out and replenished his soul. Outside, the winds picked up. He couldn't hear them for the music, but the tough little spiderweb shook, rattled, and rolled up there in its corner. Lightning split the sky, and his eyes were drawn to the cemetery just for a second.

Of course, they focused on the freshly covered plot beneath the great oak. A shiver passed through him as he thought about the body down there, newly rehomed in its casket beneath the dirt.

He pulled away, focusing on anything that his eyes met. This time, it was the bottle of bourbon. He considered taking another swig and decided against it. It was doing fuck all to soothe his head and, after all, it would only make tomorrow night's shift that much more drawn out if he finished the bottle now. He pushed the liquor aside as Dion's voice faded out into infinity. It sounded to Frank like rebellion slowly dying, going out on its own terms. Going out like a legend.

Then, when it was over and done and his mind had swung all the way back down to Earth again, he eyeballed the console. There were five lights on there, each one representing five callers in a queue. Usually there'd be three or four of them lit up and Frank would 'eeny, meeny, miny and moe' the shit out of that thing. Anything to keep the brain going. Anything to stem the tide of weariness.

Not this night, though. This night – he looked at his watch and found it was closing in on 3am, the witching hour – there was only one light flashing, angry and red. "Okay then," he muttered to himself. "I guess you're it, lonesome bird."

Frank pushed the button down. The familiar static buzzed inside his head, fed through the headset. "Hi there, caller," he said. "So glad to have you with us on this fine, fine evening."

Frank waited.

No response.

He frowned. "Hello? Caller... can you hear me?"

The empty airwaves whispered sweet, static nothings in his ear.

Shit. "Sorry folks. I think we're having a few issues with reception here. No doubt due to that ferocious storm out there. It's kicking up one hell of a fright. Well... such is the way of things. Tell you what, folks, how about I play you a little favorite of mine from 1967 by the 13th Floor Elevators. It's called Slip Inside This House. That'll tide us over while we try to —"

A voice came down the line. Female. Lilting.

It sounded very far off, seeming to drift into his psyche not through the wires and wizardry of his top-line headset, but from somewhere *further*; riding a different frequency; distant, muted, near imperceptible. Frank squinted, pushing the headset tight onto his ears so he could better pick up the woman's words. "Sorry, darlin'... I'm having a hard time hearing you. Could you repeat that?"

A second passed. Then another. The faint static crackled in his ears, sounding like logs in a fire, succumbing to hungry flame.

He waited a few seconds more.

Nothing.

It seemed the call had dropped.

And yet...

Frank had the sense that the caller was still there. He could hear nothing, but the air felt heavy somehow, weighted by a human presence.

"Can you hear me?" he asked again.

A voice answered. Still distant, no more than a whisper, but closer: "Please..." it said. And that was all.

Had the woman said more? Had the storm's effect on the signal stolen her words? It made sense.

But Frank didn't think so. Frank had the sense that her one word was all she'd offered, and it sent a chill up his spine. She sounded lost, desperate.

He leaned into the mic. "Are you okay, sweetheart? You don't sound so good."

Frank waited. Then, across the unknown miles that separated his studio from the mysterious guest, the woman repeated herself. It cut through the silence so clearly this time that Frank almost gasped aloud. The pleading tone in the woman's voice was unmistakable and more than a little disquieting, but that wasn't what truly had Frank on edge.

He recognized the voice.

He was sure of it.

Though only one word was spoken, something in the inflection... something in the pronunciation. He swallowed hard, doing his best to ignore the dread that was creeping up on him fast.

It's your imagination, Frank.

Maintain, you silly son of a bitch.

When he spoke, his throat felt parched. "I'm sorry hon. Tell you what... I'm gonna put you on hold for a second, fiddle around with these here wires and whatnots on my desk and get right back to you. Soon, we'll be playing your song, whatever it may be."

He released the button with more haste than he was comfortable doing so. There'd been no need to tinker with the wires. The line was obviously fine as she'd spoken far clearer just now. The truth of it was, Frank needed a moment, free of the call. Which made no damn sense. It was nothing more than a bust call mixing and making merry with his over-tired brain, taking the banal and spicing it up with a cruel dose of the horrors. On nights like this, when the harvest moon seemed to pulsate and the winds howled like despairing wolves, a man was prone to having his mind run off with his common sense.

No one could blame it.

But he was *sure* he recognized that voice.

And *that*, of course, was impossible.

"What's *wrong* with me?" he asked the empty room.

Suddenly, though she was on hold, he was sure the woman on the other end of the line could still hear his words.

She was listening.

There you go again, dumbshit. Letting your imagination do your thinking for you.

"Bone weary is all," he muttered, casting a quick glance up at the clock. Two minutes past three. Still half an hour of airtime left. He willed the clock's hands to turn faster than reality would afford. When that failed, he eyed the console like it was a sentient thing.

"Fuck you," he whispered, unsure whether addressing himself, the console, or the strange woman who sounded so much like the girl he'd known.

He reached for the button.

Don't press it.

Frank paused with his finger resting above the console, frozen mid-motion by the uncanny sensation that something was very, very wrong here.

You're letting this whole situation eat you up, he scolded himself.

This situation, or the booze.

Maybe both.

Outside, the wind howled its dirge. Trees creaked painfully, bent by the elements.

Don't press it.

His face burned with shame. He was acting like a fucking kindergartner.

This shit was getting ridiculous.

He looked down at his frozen finger, hovering above the button.

The flashing red light was a devil's eye, winking at him knowingly.

Go on... *do it*, it said.

"Fuck you," he repeated, now squarely aiming the angry remark towards himself. This was no more than yet another bout of the late-night terrors, more severe than his previous slips into superstition and childish notions, yet no less idiotic.

Maybe the caller will hang up if I hold on a moment longer, the child inside him countered.

And why would you want that? he railed. You're a fucking radio host. It's your *job* to answer these insomniacs and play them their shitty songs. Get your shit all the way together and *press the button.*

Outside, the autumn winds wailed, rustling the dying leaves that clung to skeletal branches down there in the cemetery. Some leaves, dead and withered and carried on that sour October wind, spattered across the windowpane, dirtying the glass, clinging there like muddy, oversized fingerprints. The low carpet of fog that lay upon the old graveyard swirled on the air, obscuring headstones, then settled, inches above the grass where the dead slept.

Press the goddam thing! Frank told himself.

Deep breath.

A countdown... one, two, three.

He pressed the button.

The red-lit eye closed at last, and the familiar low-level static hummed in his ears through a headset that felt heavy as stone on his head.

"Sorry about that, ma'am. Hopefully now we can — "

"Please...play...my song." The woman sounded haggard, worn out, anguished. Yet she sounded no less familiar.

Frank composed himself, pushed his fear deep down. "I'd... I'd be happy to. And what song is that?"

A soft, cynical chuckle echoed down the line.

Cynical? Or was that malice he detected in the strangely hollow laughter?

"Play… the… song… I… love." She sounded closer still. Her words seemed to reach out and touch him. The gruesome caress of a spider's web on naked skin. Frank shuddered at the sensation. She went on. "The… one…they played… for… me."

"And what song is that?" he asked, afraid of the tremor he detected in his own voice.

"They… all… cried…" She sighed sadly. "When they played… my song."

Frank peered out into the night, lost for a response.

His gaze settled again on the gravestone beneath the old oak tree; the one with the stone angel perched atop it and the still-fresh soil from the previous week's burial. He could still see the mourners down there, huddled together in the rain, clutching each other close under black umbrellas, eyes wreathed in bitter tears from

crying.

Something black rustled its tenebrous wings in his gut.

It felt like terror.

27

Laughter, guttural and wet, poured down the line, no longer the sound of a woman. This was the empty, withered rasping of a nightmare witch, a crone.

A dead thing.

"Oh... how they cried. How they all... cried," the low, corrupted voice sighed. The expulsion of breath was a death rattle.

Frank's mind reeled. "I'm sorry. I think I have to—"

"All but *you,* Frank..." the dark thing said.

Frank tore the headset off and flung it across the room. It clattered to the floor. He pushed hard on the console's button, cutting the terrible, hideous caller off at last.

From the headset, malignant laughter oozed like a horror birthed from a child's nightmare realm.

This isn't happening.

"Play... my... song."

He lunged from the console in a mad dash and brought his boot down hard on the headset. It smashed beneath his feet.

"Leave me alone!" he screamed.

A lifetime passed in the splinter of a second, and all was silent.

Wild eyed and panic stricken, Frank flopped back into his chair. He reached for the bourbon with shaking hands, brought it to his lips and swallowed.

Stillness. Only the constant rattle of rain on glass and the yawning of the tortured trees beyond it. Tears filled his eyes. "No more!" he swore to the bottle and its swirling contents. "No fucking more." Even as he spoke, he brought it up again for another deep swig. The bourbon burned his throat going down but could do nothing to burn away the razor's edge of panic deeper down inside him. For the first time in life, Frank understood the stark, black terror that came with the knowledge that one was losing their mind.

She's gone. Gone! He told himself. Lynnette only exists in your mind. You saw to that. You saw to it, once and for all.

The moment played out in his mind's eye, feverish; with the all too crisp malignance of a detox tremor.

Lynnette... swaying drunkenly around their hallway, gracelessly pirouetting in an alcoholic stupor. Her once beautiful, firm figure reduced to fatty, drooping rubble by years of hard liquor. Naked tits flapping like two punctured balloons, arms riddled with varicose veins, smiling her lopsided idiot smile as she crashes into the paintings that adorn the walls, toppling them to the floor. The music thunders, crashing through his addled, hangover-ridden skull with all the blunt force of a sledgehammer, rattling his insides as he stumbles down the hall, half-sleeping.

"What the fuck are you doing? It's the middle of the fucking night!" he roars.

"Dance with me, baby" she shouts in a befuddled slur. "It's my favorite song!"

A mist, red as freshly drawn blood, descends over his mind as he watches her spin and twirl and giggle and cheer. "I *love* this song!" she hollers.

He's moving down the hallway to where she stands before he even realizes he's doing so. She reaches for him. "Dance with me!" She stumbles backwards at the head of the stairs, almost going down but regaining her balance at the very last moment as drunks are apt to do. "Dance with me!"

Frank draws closer to the woman he once loved and now, god help him, hates. She grins, drool spilling over her once luscious lips and down her chin.

"I have work tomorrow, you bitch!" he shouts.

Then he pushes.

That's all it takes.

One little push.

Her alcohol ravaged body does the rest of the work for him.

For the briefest of moments, sobriety seems to flash behind her eyes like a bolt of unheralded lightning. With it comes understanding.

Then she's falling, toppling head over heels down the long staircase like a discarded marionette. She never screams, and he's grateful for it. The sound of her snapping bones is deafening enough.

Then it's over.

Her song still blares from the sound system, but Lynette dances no more.

From the bottom of the staircase, she stares up at him with eyes already fading, her once pretty head twisted around at an impossible angle, blood mixing with the drool from her open maw like a drunkard's clumsily applied lipstick.

Then she is gone.

The funeral had been tough. Though her death was immediately ruled to be accidental (no small surprise, given her reputation around town as one of the hopelessly fallen), there had still been the accusatory stares as they lowered her into the ground. Friends and family who, while accepting of the coroner's results, still harbored the tiniest of doubts about what had truly occurred that horrible, tragic night. None were outright in their suspicions, but it was there, behind the eyes, in the quick, angry glances his way while he watched her coffin sink low. He'd tried to muster up some tears, play to the crowd. It looked bad... her partner stood there with dry eyes while all around him moaned and wept, but he just couldn't manage it.

But the funeral was over. That damnable plot of land down there by the oak tree would soon turn green. Birds would nestle in the old tree's branches, singing their songs of love and shitting on that ridiculous ceramic angel, and no one would ever be the wiser.

She was dead. She was gone.

But the voice of the caller, first youthful, then haggard and broken, had been hers.

Only in your mind, Frank.

Only in your mind.

Frank laid the now-empty bourbon bottle down on the desk and let the memory, and the shame, peel away.

Downstairs, the front door opened with an agonized squeal.

The wind?

Had to be.

You just forgot to lock it, he told himself.

But that wasn't so.

Frank turned to the window. He had no idea what he was waiting for until it came.

The whiplash of lightning lit up the old cemetery in brilliant white light. Only for a moment, but a moment was enough.

In the angry flash, Frank saw her plot. Saw the freshly toiled earth cast aside around the reopened hole; the open, empty casket, shimmering in the rain. Muddy footprints pressed into the soil around the black pit in which she'd rested...

waited.

Behind him, the undeniable thud of feet on stairs. Something coming. Something drawing closer, one step at a time, moving with hideous intent. He spun around, stared dumbstruck at the door, frozen in mute horror, unable to act, to run, to fight. Only able to wait.

The footsteps ceased atop the landing.

The doorknob turned.

"I'm sorry. I'm so sorry," he moaned as the door swung wide and from the shadows beyond a voice, hollow with hatred and decay, answered. "Then dance with me, Frank. Dance with me, down in the darkness."

Frank never felt the warm piss run down his leg. Nor did he hear his own screams as she staggered into the light with filthy, already rotting arms outstretched. Her head hung low on her ruined neck, yet she managed to meet his eyes with a dead stare. The mortuary's makeup artist has done their work well; had made her up to look like one of the living. Now that work had been reduced to a cruel parody of life. The makeup ran and mixed with already slewing flesh that writhed with the worms living therein.

"Dance with me," she croaked. Her rotten fingers wrapped around his shoulders and her broken, filthy nails clawed his back.

Despite the ruination of her neck, the thing that had been Lynette raised its head and drew its black, moldering lips close to his own. Stitches snapped, tearing through the decaying lips as they parted wide, exhaling a stinking cloud of sickly-sweet rot. In the dark maw, maggots feverishly writhed, a thousand tiny mouths feasting on the succulent, putrefying meat.

"Dance with me forever," the dead thing whispered.

Their lips met. The living flood poured from her mouth into his own; a seething, hungry wave that filled his gullet and stole his breath. From the console, a song kicked up and music filled the air. That song she loved. The one she'd danced to. The one she'd died to. The one that made everyone cry as they laid her in her grave and bid her farewell.

Everyone but him.

The horror that had been Lynette's song filled his screaming, shattering mind.

Frank finally cried.

He cried all the way down into the darkness.

The End

And the Dead Shall Perish

By

Mike Duke

Young Elek Gabor clutched the broken piece of Ash wood against his torso. A thick black ooze sloughed off the jagged end as his chest heaved up and down. Desperate to stay hidden from the ghouls, he struggled to control his breathing, slow his racing heart and the rapid inhalations laboring to provide oxygen to his adrenaline flooded muscles. He didn't dare move from his position. The creatures were in an uproar now, shrieking, barking, growling as they hunted for him. He could hear them skulking outside the toolshed, claws skittering over cobblestone, rotten flesh padding along the grassy ground nearby, squelching as they went.

The worst sounds, though, came from noses snuffling the air like pigs searching for truffles.

*****

The ghouls could smell the blood of a human with ease. Elek saw this firsthand over the last few days since the creatures emerged. A fresh crimson flow was irresistible to them. If you bled, for any reason, it was like ringing the dinner bell or chumming waters for sharks.

They would swarm. They would feed. There was slim hope of escape.

The most delectable morsels were preserved and delivered to their master. Young boys. Infants. Petite tween girls. Any virgin flesh would suffice. Their master drained their gifts dry and tossed the corpses to his servants. They desecrated the still warm bodies, satisfying their lecherous delights before consuming the flesh. The ghouls slurped and smacked their lips, gnawing bones clean of meat and gristle before crunching them into pieces and sucking out the marrow. The tender infants were wolfed down, gobbling them up with a rabid fury.

At night, the threat was twice as deadly. Sleepless fiends lurked a hand's breadth out of striking range from the ghouls, darting in to lick up blood and scraps then scamper away before the ghouls had an opportunity to lash out. But during the day, the fiends feasted. They alone were capable of dwelling beneath the sun. At first light, the ghouls followed their master back to Sumegi temeto graveyard, where they burrowed deep beneath the ground.

Elek was unsure whether they had dug holes beneath the graves or whether, perhaps, there was a hidden tunnel system of sorts. He only knew they fled the daylight while the fiends continued to hunt the dwindling humans left in the city, hounding their every movement and denying most the opportunity to make any productive provisions for the coming night or to reach Sumeg Castle. It was the only safe place, seated high on the hill looking over the entire city of Sumeg, Hungary. The people there had made siege preparations, and so far, they were holding off their hungry enemies.

Many of the villagers fled to the churches for sanctuary when the outbreak first began. Neither the ghouls nor their master dared tread upon the sacred ground. But the fiends had no such limitations. Once the master drove his teeth into a human's flesh, drained much of their blood, and made them drink his own, they obeyed him and showed no fear of trespassing within God's holy temples. These fiends assaulted every church with a relentless zeal, forcing the people of Sumeg to fend off their bloodthirsty attackers round the clock: fiends by day and both ghouls and fiends by night.

During the day, they ransacked houses and forced their way into the cathedrals, dragging the sick and frail out into the streets, corralling them in the public square until sunset. Any healthy ones they overcame were theirs to consume. At nightfall, when the master clambered forth from the ground, he slaked his thirst on the weak and helpless victims, then fed them his blood to create more fiendish servants ready to devour their fellow man.

Elek had observed all this. Being a small skinny lad, he was able to squeeze into nooks and crannies and stay out of sight, slipping from house to house to find food and drink. By day, he kept his whole body covered, including hands and head with gloves and a ski mask, careful not to even scratch himself against anything while crawling and hiding. The fiends' sense of smell was not as keen as the ghouls, but it was enough to present a significant threat. At night, he bundled up and hid within attics or church belfries.

From high in a belfry, he had watched the master move about the city. He was a gigantic man, easily eight feet tall, slipping through the shadows with an unexpected gracefulness, rarely exposing himself, even beneath the moonlight. When he was prepared to feed, the ghouls brought their offerings to him. Pale skin marred by dark sores glistened for a moment as clawed hands grasped his next meal and drew them into the darkness where he fed. Elek swore he saw the silhouette of an enormous jaw unhinge and open wide, a mouth full of fangs outlined by a glint of moonlight before the master chomped into the sacrifice offered by his servants.

*****

Elek sat motionless, listening intently to the creatures outside the toolshed. Their fearful noises faded

41

as the monsters moved off toward the castle and away from him. He relaxed. He had killed one fiend with a makeshift stake through the heart. It wasn't a vampire, but it wasn't human any longer either.

Though, Elek had never considered Mr. Gyula, the librarian, to be properly human at all. The man possessed no sense of humor, no soul or animus. No distinguishing characteristics except a cold, reptilian gaze he fixed young people with that reeked of hunger. From what Elek had seen, the man appeared to possess perverse proclivities for children, both boys and girls. Elek knew he, himself, was not the only boy to have turned down a dead-end aisle, eager to acquire a book, only to find Mr. Gyula standing there within arm's reach of the very literary treasure they desired to retrieve. Elek had frozen on many occasions, standing still and unsure, uncomfortable with his teacher's disturbing attention. The man seemed driven by a devious intent which caused him to focus on Elek's body. Elek felt much like a gazelle staring into a crocodile's eyes by the waterhole it longs to drink from. At times he abandoned his prize to find another. On other occasions he lunged in, seized the book and scampered away with a "Thank you Mr. Gyula" cast over his shoulder.

Once turned into a fiend, Mr. Gyula threw off any semblance of humanity. Elek had seen the man perform vile deeds while feeding, both before and after the victims died. When the former professor drew near to his hiding place, Elek gripped the broken shovel handle and leaped down from the roof of a shed, driving it into Gyula's heart from the back. Elek figured that alive or undead, that should do the trick.

"*Unless the man is a zombie,*" he had thought with a fair amount of concern.

Mr. Gyula wailed with his dying breath and ceased moving.

"*Thank God, they're not zombies!*" raced through the boy's mind as he withdrew the weapon. He darted inside the tool shed and jammed a piece of wood against the door handle. Once the door was secured, he wedged himself under part of a workbench and waited. It was there he managed to fall asleep once his monstrous pursuers had moved on.

*****

Elek awoke to the sound of screams nearby. A female's, at first, then a male's. He slid from under the bench, trying not to make a sound and eased toward the entrance. Elek removed the board and inched the door open. He felt a jarring impact from the other side, and it flew open, shoving him off balance. He tipped over backwards and fell away from the doorway. For a moment his stomach plummeted into a yawning chasm. He knew he was dead. A second later his fears dissipated as two people rushed in and slammed the door behind them.

A young man pinned his back to the entrance to prevent the creatures from barging in if they found them. It was a futile precaution. Elek knew the boy alone would not stop ghoul or fiend. The girl whined through her teeth, whimpering, lips pressed together tight, hands clamped over her mouth.

"Szonja," the young man whispered. "You must be quiet!"

Elek made out the two figures by the pale moonlight creeping in through the tiny window above the workbench. The girl appeared older than Elek but not by much. The male was likely her big brother. Blood trickled down his forehead and over his left cheek.

"You're bleeding," Elek stated, a blunt declaration that surprised both newcomers.

Szonja's hands muffled her shriek as she whirled around to see where the voice came from. The young man didn't make a noise but nearly jumped out of his skin. Elek was thankful the girl smothered her cry.

"You can't stay here," Elek finished.

"Wh… we… what?" the brother stuttered out.

"You're bleeding," Elek repeated, matter of fact, as if it were the most obvious thing in this world gone mad. "You can't stay here. They'll find us."

The young man looked at him confused.

"You mean you don't know?" Elek asked. The young man shook his head in response, perplexed.

"The ghouls can smell blood as well as any shark," Elek explained. "You must leave now, or you'll lead them right to us. I'll die, and she'll die too," Elek said, jabbing his finger at Szonja. "Now, get out!" Elek commanded in a hushed tone.

"No Miklos!" the girl cried, gripping the boy's arm. "Brother, you cannot leave me," she pleaded, her face earnest, unable to accept this new development.

The thought of going outside with those creatures terrified Miklos, but his instinct to protect his sister overrode the near immobilizing fear. He grabbed Szonja by the shoulders and shook her gently.

"I love you," he told her, tears in his eyes. "Do not follow me."

Miklos turned to Elek. "Hide her," he commanded then threw open the door and dashed away into the night. Elek scrambled forward and shut the door.

Pulling a lighter from his pocket, he clicked it on and cupped his free hand to direct the light. He moved it all around, scanning to make sure Miklos hadn't spilled any blood inside the tool shed. Satisfied there were no drops present, he turned the flame on Szonja and assessed her.

"Are you hurt?" Elek asked.

She shook her head and moaned a simple "No."

"OK." Elek jammed the piece of wood beneath the door handle once more. "Be still and be silent," he ordered her. "The ghouls cannot see. Their eyes are milky white orbs. They can detect blood, though, and they have excellent hearing. The others, the changed, they can see but have no advantage I've noticed, except being harder to kill than the average man and they can tread on holy ground. But they no longer possess their humanity. They are fiends. Driven by godless appetites and servants to their master. You understand?"

Szonja nodded and wiped tears from her eyes.

A terrible scream broke the silent night. Szonja let loose a gasp and clasped both hands over her mouth again. She sat on the floor with a thud, her legs weak. He knew it must be her brother.

Elek remained kneeling, muscles tensed, barely breathing, afraid to inhale more than a fraction of air at a time. The screams turned into shrieks mixed with bellowing wails. Miklos's agonizing cries carried on the night air and refused to cease. The ghouls and fiends were in no rush to finish the girl's brother. Elek turned his head to see Szonja. Both hands covered her ears, and she was squeezing her eyes shut. She rocked back and forth, unable to remain still, arms twitching, shaking as if with palsy.

"Stop moving," Elek whispered, but she couldn't hear him. He leaned toward her, reached out, stretching until his fingertips touched her knee. She jerked, eyelids flying open, her gaze wild and full of shock, barely capable of focusing on Elek. He held up one finger to his lips, then lowered his hand, raising and lifting it twice to encourage her to calm down and not move.

It was at that moment they heard the snuffling noises.

Elek's blood ran cold. His bladder released, and he had to squeeze his muscles to stop the flow. He leaned away from Szonja, returning to a point of balance. Holding his breath, he looked around for a weapon. There was a combo hoe and cultivator hanging on the wall beside the door on his side.

The snuffling grew louder … closer. The sound of their noses rubbing against the shed blared in his head, the volume amplified by his terror. He grabbed the end of the hoe handle and with a measured, gentle effort, lifted it off the rack without a noise and lowered it into both his hands. His fingers curled about the wood, gripping it for battle.

Nails scrabbled against the bottom of the door, scratching, digging, clawing. First with a tentative probing action, and next with a voracious vigor.

Oh God, no, Elek thought.

He waved at Szonja in a panic, catching her attention. He pointed at her eyes with his index and middle finger then at his back and forth. She stared at him with concern. He mouthed the words for her to see, exaggerating his lip movement.

"You're bleeding," he told her.

Szonja's head shook with denial then halted with alarming suddenness as her conviction faltered. Her eyes grew big and incredulous. Her face went slack as a palpable dread weighed her jaw down and stretched the skin over her cheeks tight. She looked down, one hand going to her groin. She felt a sticky dampness and raised her head back up to meet Elek's horrified gaze.

"Oh God, no" she muttered silently, pure terror taking over her body. Her face contorted in panic. Fear gripped her heart and she implored, begged.

"Oh God, no. Please, no. No, no, no, no, no!"

BANG!

Murderous hands slammed into the door, shaking it.

BANG!

Again, they struck the wooden door. The splintering sound jarred his senses, making him jump.

He stared at Szonja.

"I can't help you," he mouthed to her and stared, cold, devoid of empathy.

What inkling of hope she thought she had vanished in an instant. Szonja's face filled with despair, her head shaking side to side and bobbling about as if at sea, rolling with the waves. Her eyes revealed the mounting hysteria stampeding through both her mind and flesh and the pang of abandonment was painted in broad, blood drained strokes across her paling cheeks.

BANG! BANG! BANG!

The creatures attacked the barrier standing between them and their feast with relentless force. The doorframe shattered and the door swung wide. Elek jumped behind it, holding the cultivator hoe in front of him, back pinned against the wall, the door touching the toes of his shoes.

Szonja fell fetal, and the ghouls descended on her, filling the tool shed. Clawed hands with fetid, sticky, moist skin grasped her every limb, twisted their fingers in her hair, scooped between her legs and carried her out of the toolshed above their heads. They jumped and danced and cavorted, making whooping hoots and frenzied infernal ululations announcing the prize they had acquired for their lord and master.

Elek stood stock still, incapable of movement. He felt confident he was dead, at first, but seconds later it was obvious the ghouls didn't see him, and they wouldn't sniff him out since he wasn't bleeding. If he remained in hiding, he might live.

There's nothing I can do for her, he told himself. *There's nothing I can do. I'm a boy. A scrawny, twelve-year-old boy. I can't save her. I'll die if I go out there now... I'll die...*

Elek struggled to not think about the horrific fate soon to befall Szonja but garnered no success. He had seen it happen to others. The master would lift her off the ground by her hair, plunge his fangs into her neck, and glut his vampiric hunger on her virgin blood. She'd kick weakly, like gazelle beneath a leopard's jaws. She'd squirm and try to scream but make little noise. When the end came, her feet would twitch and kick no more. After the master finished feasting, he'd toss her corpse to the waiting ghouls. Each would defile her lifeless body and then, together, they would devour her bones and all.

He knew these things were inevitable. He was not powerful enough to stop them. Yet, Elek writhed within, dirty and ashamed. A man did not act like this; did not cower in the face of evil. His father did not cringe in terror. No. He died a man, four nights ago fighting the ghouls to save Elek, his mother, and the neighbor's daughter, Anna, who was helping Elek with his math homework. His dad fought and perished to give them an opportunity to live.

How can you just let her die? Elek asked himself.

By doing nothing, another part of his brain answered, *just like you did with your mother and Anna.*

The words convicted him, reminded him of his cowardice and guilt. He had hidden in a closet, peaking out through a crack in the door, shadows and silence his refuge, as his mother and Anna were dragged from the house they had taken shelter inside. The sounds of the fiends raping his mother on the front porch returned to Elek and then the sloppy noises of their feasting. Jagged teeth rending flesh, tearing large chunks away; lips smacking, throats wolfing them down with a greedy glee. Worst of all, they did not wait to feast. They gorged themselves throughout her violation. But Elek's mother had refused to scream, refused to leave Elek with those memories. It was horrible enough without them. If the cries of his mother were added to the cacophony echoing in his mind, in every silent moment of each day and night, Elek might have gone mad and taken his own life. Because Elek knew he was no man. He had done nothing. Hiding was his great battleplan. Cowardice his shield.

Don't do this again, he told himself. *It's not right.*

He glanced around the tool shed. His eyes spotted the broken shovel handle covered in black ooze. He also noticed a five-gallon jug of gasoline and rags.

Maybe…

A possibility occurred to Elek. Perhaps he wouldn't win, perhaps he couldn't save Szonja, but perhaps, against all odds, he might do both.

"Nothing ventured, nothing gained," he thought.

Elek gathered the necessary gear and prepared them in a hurry before peeking out to make sure the coast was clear. Satisfied, he set off at a trot, moving as quick as the load of items he carried would allow.

Every rustling noise or hoot of an owl startled him and made his head snap from side to side in search of any potential threat. He continued to follow the ghoulish laughter and sounds of celebration, closing on them in haste. It appeared they were making their way to the intersection of Kossuth Lajos and Martirok Utja, in front of the Kisfaludy Vendeghaz hotel. Taking a parallel street, he flanked them.

Elek knew his village well. He was more than capable of predicting where the shadows would lie and the streetlights shine; where the ghouls' master was likely to emerge, creeping up to the edge of darkness. Elek turned down an alley that came out beside the gymnasium, one building over from where he believed the master would show himself. He moved from one plot of darkness to another, shot across the street, and squatted between two cars parked on the side of the hotel. It was an advantageous position for his longshot plan.

He watched the ghouls and fiends hurry toward the hotel. They were in a frenzy now. Their brutish grunts, squawks, roars, and howls formed a hideous and discordant melody that drowned out all else nearby.

The unholy creatures placed Szonja on the cobblestone in front of the entrance to the hotel and burst forth in jubilant revelry. They capered, pranced, frolicked, and danced, expecting their lord's arrival with glee. The pending bestial delights would satisfy their concupiscent appetites. They would have their fill of fleshly pleasures and feast on Szonja's sweet corpse flesh together. The ghoul's perverse expectancies soared to festive heights. They sniffed, snuffled, and snorted, as if trying to taste the virgin blood on the air itself; eyes rolling back with rapturous glee, pale, venous white orbs fluttering beneath the moon above. When the fiends drew near Szonja, the ghouls leapt on them, inflicting vicious, snapping bites and claw wounds that raked deep furrows in the skin.

The fiends fled, scurrying to escape further injury. They hovered on the periphery, stalked about on all fours and whined, staring at Szonja, longing to join the ghouls in the coming lecherous debauchery.

Elek noticed a change in the shadows by the fiends. Beneath a group of trees near to where Szonja lay sobbing, something blotted out the night, obstructed all light. It was as if a great form moved to eclipse the midnight gloom, casting a black shade over the darkness itself.

The master, Elek thought.

The ghouls purred with bowed heads then shrieked in joy and creeped toward Szonja, chuckling as they glanced from one to another.

Now!

Elek lit the gas-soaked rag stuffed in the large fuel can. *Be the man*, he told himself. *Be your father's son, for god's sake.*

He took a step, spun, circling to generate more force, and threw the container with both hands into the edge of the shadows. It exploded, illuminating the entire area as if by daylight. Liquid fire showered the area, dousing the fiends along with their master.

Elek saw the ancient monstrosity in that moment, diabolical and obscene, revolting and terrifying all at once. The master's face drew his eyes, commanded them like a hypnotist to stare at the beast, but Elek refused to continue looking. He did not gawk or stand idle, frozen by paralyzing dread. Instead, broken shovel handle gripped tight, Elek ran straight at the vampire lord.

Stripped of his shadowy cloak, the master's pallid, cadaverous flesh was exposed for any to see. Mottled with dark sores, its skin stretched taut over dense muscles and an inhumanly large bone structure. He rose to his full height, mouth even with the bottom edge of a first story roof, arms shielding his eyes as the fuel and flames spread up his legs and torso. Jagged talons grew from all his fingers and toes, and leathery maggot-white wings draped down to his knees. The gasoline conflagration had set his whole body ablaze.

The fiends dashed about in blind panic, like flaming bumper cars, bouncing into several of the ghouls and setting them on fire as well before careening into another comrade or a tree or car. One of them banged into Szonja in the confusion setting her clothes alight. The fiends and burning ghouls shrieked and clawed at their charring skin, spastically flopping on the ground or running through the streets as if they might escape the flames consuming their flesh.

Szonja's coat burned. Elek saw it, but he could not stop for her now. To do so would be their ruin. He sprinted for the master, hoping to close the distance before the monster took flight or realized Elek was upon him. The bedlam Elek's oversized Molotov cocktail had created was working wonderfully.

The master extended and retracted his wings, slapping his legs with them as he roared with a primal rage Elek never fathomed existed.

"Dear God, guide my hand," Elek prayed out loud at the last second as he jumped up on the hood of a car. As he approached the point of no return, and clambered onto the roof of the vehicle, he watched the beast's body rotate, the wings part and drop at the perfect moment, opening the way for Elek's attack as if by divine invitation.

Elek leapt into the air, a tiny David throwing himself at Goliath. Both hands clutching the shovel handle, he plunged it into the heart of the vampire lord with all his might and mass. He released the stake and dropped to the ground, but while still airborne a wing lashed out, buffeting him across the street where he hit the cobblestone and rolled, tumbling until a car tire stopped him, the impact knocking the wind out of him.

A deafening screech pierced his ears, a sound of fury and pain, the cry filled with the fear of defeat and perhaps even death. Elek didn't swivel his head to admire his handiwork, however. There was no time. He scrambled to his feet, wheezing for air, took off his coat, and struck Szonja with it to put out the flames kindling upon her clothing. Once he brought them under control, he peeled the jacket right off her back and arms.

"C'mon!" he yelled at her and wheezed again, sucking in more air now than a few seconds before.

Grabbing a wrist, he dragged Szonja to her feet, his legs pumping like a sled dog, digging. They ran, ran and didn't waste a moment rubbernecking. He was focused on getting his wind back and channeling every ounce of oxygen into flight. Elek's heart soared at the sound of the master's death wail and his lips parted in a malicious smile from ear to ear. But then he heard another noise and his hopes sank. The murderous cries of the surviving ghouls pierced the night. Those not consumed by the fire pursued Elek and Szonja with a malevolent zeal.

Elek and Szonja's legs carried them faster than they had ever run in their lives, arms pumping, hands clasped together, Elek refusing to let go, and Szonja desperate to not falter and fall behind.

Elek led the way. Down Kossuth Lajos St., a right onto Szent Istvan ter, and from there it was a full throttle race the last few blocks to reach the Franciscan monastery. Holy ground.

Their hearts pounded like jackhammers and their lungs worked like a blacksmith's bellows, sucking air in and blowing out at a breakneck pace. The hoots and howls and furious shrieks of the ghouls drew closer and closer, inches every second at first and then feet the longer they ran.

Don't look back, Elek commanded himself. *Don't look back!*

But Elek couldn't resist. He cast a momentary glance over his shoulder, searching for a glimpse of anything that might inform him as to how dire their circumstances were.

"Oh, God!" he squalled. The mob of hell spawn pursuers were a hundred feet away, if that.

"What?" Szonja shouted in response to Elek's exclamatory cry.

"Don't look back!" he yelled at Szonja. "Whatever you do, *don't* look back!"

Szonja was too scared to see how close to death they were. The fear fueled her final burst. The church grounds were near. If they reached sacred soil, the ghouls could not follow them. Elek squeezed Szonja's hand tighter and bled his muscles dry for every ounce of effort they could give him.

The skittering of claws and thumping of bloated soles against the cobblestone road gained on them despite their heroic efforts. Their flight seemed hopeless, but they refused to give up. Elek was sure he felt cool fetid breath on the nape of his neck. The hairs stood on end. His shoulders scrunched upward in fear of death a second before they crossed over onto the church grounds. A stinging, searing pain bit into his left arm and it went limp. The smell of burning flesh flickered in his nostrils then vanished.

Elek clutched his upper arm with his good hand but didn't dare look back this time. He kept running, straight for the entrance. There was a high-arched entryway secured with a wrought-iron gate close to seven feet tall. Elek studied it as he rushed forward. There was room for someone to fit above it. As they reached it, Elek pushed Szonja up first with his good arm.

"Climb! Climb!" he yelled at her. As he helped push her upward, he turned around to see if he might die.

The ghouls were spitting mad. Some of them ripped signposts from the earth and cast them down while others lashed out at cars and building walls, flailing at everything they bumped into. One stood shaking his burning hand, trying to extinguish the holy flame that set it ablaze when it reached for the boy, crossing the threshhold. The ghouls roared, bellowed, howled, groaned, and, at last, let out a ferocious ululation that made Elek's heart nearly stop. But they did not step foot on the church grounds. They did not dare touch this consecrated site. That meant eternal death. It would consume them, and they knew it.

Elek noticed with much relief that there were no fiends mixed in with the ghouls. He hoped it meant the master had perished, and the fiends fell with him. If their creator did not survive, there was no one to sustain their half-dead flesh. If so, this was a godsend. Though he knew they might simply have burned up. Either way, with the rising sun, the surviving ghouls would have to flee back to the graveyard, retreat underground. And without their master, they might not return tonight to stalk the streets of Sumeg.

"Hurry," Szonja urged him. "Get inside!"

Elek turned away from the beasts, pulled himself up with one arm and managed to crawl over the gate and half drop, half fall to the stone floor. Szonja embraced his thin frame and clutched him to her with a tenacity birthed from a desperate hopelessness transformed into victory, snatched from the maw of hell itself. A powerful cathartic explosion of emotions surged forth from her heart and directly into Elek's soul.

Elek knew his father was proud of him, looking down from heaven. He did not value his life above those in need. He did what was right. The evil they faced tonight drew out the man within Elek, the man his dad raised.

Wrapping an arm over her shoulder, he squeezed Szonja to his chest. He sensed a baptism of bliss descend upon him, warm and euphoric. Elek looked toward the heavens and whispered to his God.

"Truly, you are Jehovah-Mephalti. The Lord my Deliverer."

"Amen to that," Szonja muttered in agreement and released her hold on Elek. She raised her gaze to meet his, took his face in her hands and kissed him on the forehead. "Thank you," she said, tears filling her eyes, a hitch catching in her voice. "Thank you for not leaving me to die."

Elek's cheeks would have blushed it they were not already so pale. He was unable to say a word, partly for fear of crying himself and partly due to his brain becoming wispy, thin and disconnected.

"Oh my god," Szonja said, "You're pale as a ghost. What's wrong?" She took a step back and held him at arm's length. She immediately saw the crimson stain stretching down his left side, the flow of blood running from the four deep lacerations cutting through Elek's left bicep and around the outside of his upper arm.

Szonja ripped a piece of material from the hem of her shirt and pressed it against the wound.

"I need to sit down," Elek informed her and lowered himself to the ground. The bleeding was slowing. The ghoul's claws had not reached the inner arm where the arteries run.

"Who's there?" a voice called out from within the church. "Have the fiends returned?" another asked.

"The fiends are dead, and the master too!" Szonja called out. "But my friend is injured and needs your help."

Szonja held pressure and smiled down at Elek, who had decided it was best to lay down when the edges of his vision started drawing in, blackness lurking at the periphery.

"I'll call sister Mary," someone called out. "She'll know what to do."

Szonja patted Elek's cheek with one hand.

"Hey," she said.

Elek's eyes blinked once then opened most of the way.

"Yeah?" he asked.

"Just making sure you're still with me," Szonja said. "Can't let my hero die on me."

She smiled and he returned the expression.

"It's going to be ok," she consoled him.

"I know," he said, looking into her emerald eyes, content.

A large man approached.

"Let's get him to sister Mary's office," the man said then bent down to lift Elek to his feet. With the man's help and Szonja maintaining pressure on the wound, Elek made his way toward the church sanctuary and from there to sister Mary's office.

As they passed through the sanctuary, Elek looked up at the crucified Christ and then at the stained-glass window where Christ sat crowned upon a throne.

"Thank you, oh Lord," Elek said aloud, "'my strength and my refuge in the day of trouble.'"

The End

Are You the Girl with Ribbons in Her Hair?

By

Douglas Hackle

An elderly man emerged from the front door of his home, somewhere in suburban Midwestern America. Locking the door behind him, he turned to face the sun rising above the close-set houses and well-kept yards across the street. Head tilted back and nostrils flared, he took in the cool, fresh, morning air of early May. Aided by a polished wooden cane, he followed his front walk down to the sidewalk. The man was glad to be on the move again, as unseasonably cold, rainy weather had prevented him from taking his morning and evening walks for the past two days, arthritic knees be damned.

Nearly three street blocks into his constitutional, he noticed a figure approaching in the opposite direction on the sidewalk. As is the custom, the man moved closer to the right side of the pavement to allow the other to pass. He halted when he realized the approaching pedestrian—

a tall, obese man—had not observed the same courtesy. The enormous man, who essentially blocked the entire width of the sidewalk, stopped a few feet away from the elderly man.

"Mornin'," the elderly man said.

Grimacing, trembling slightly, sweat dripping in rivulets down his pimple-studded face, the obese man nervously wrung his hands. He wore thick, round glasses that greatly magnified his eyes, a multicolored propeller beanie, and an immense white t-shirt on which the barely legible words "I LOVE MY MOM AND MY GRANDPAPS" had been scrawled with black magic marker.

"Are y-y-you the g-g-girl with ribbons in her hair?" the propeller beanie man said, his voice nasal and tremulous.

The elderly man frowned, bent an ear toward the speaker. "Come again, son? My hearing's not so sharp these days."

"Are y-y-you the g-g-girl with ribbons in her hair?"

The elderly man pulled a sour face. "Am I the what?"

"The girl with ribbons in her hair."

"A girl with ribbons in her hair? Are you trying to make a joke, son?"

"Are you the girl with ribbons in her hair?"

Guessing the progression of the joke relied on him providing a yes or no response, the elderly man shook his head. "No. I'm not a girl with ribbons in her hair."

As if in sore disappointment, the propeller beanie man whimpered like a dog. He then raised his right hand in the air, the chubby fingers and thumb curving inward to form a claw shape.

"CRUSH HEAD!" the man called out before he slowly closed his fingers into a quivering fist.

As he did so, the elderly man's head imploded as if caught in the crushing grip of a giant hand. The man's dead body collapsed to the sidewalk a beat later, his bowels evacuating audibly into his pants.

Stepping around the corpse, the propeller beanie man continued on his way.

***

"Are you the girl with ribbons in her hair?" he asked the next person he encountered on the sidewalk—a seventh-grade boy running late on his way to school.

The boy eyeballed the strange man with much justified suspicion.

"Um, I'm not allowed to talk to strangers." Averting his eyes, he sidestepped onto a tree lawn to give the man a wide berth as he walked around him.

The propeller beanie man turned in place, his beady gaze following the boy like a laser sight as he passed.

"Are you the girl with ribbons in her hair?" he called after him.

Without looking back, the boy adjusted the shoulder straps of his overfilled backpack, held up a reverse middle finger, and accelerated his pace to a trot.

A pathetic, mournful whine rose in the propeller beanie man's throat. His brow furrowed into an angry "v" just as a gust of wind sent his beanie propeller into a whirring spin. The strain and pressure of the contorted grimace pasted to the man's moonlike face then caused a large, ripe pimple on his forehead to spontaneously rupture, out of which pus and a thread of blood joined with a rivulet of sweat trickling down his ample cheek, the white and red mixing to form runny pink.

Once again, the man raised a claw-like hand into the air and slowly closed it into a fist.

"CRUSH HEAD!"

***

A block away from where the boy's dead body lay, a fenced-in dog barked at the propeller beanie man's approach. Pausing at the corner of the yard where the dog stood just beyond the barrier of white vinyl pickets, the propeller beanie man glared down at the black and white border collie/Lab mix.

"Are you the girl with ribbons in her hair?" he asked.

The dog barked at him.

"Are you the girl with ribbons in her hair?"

A good judge of character, the dog growled at the man, baring its teeth.

The propeller beanie man scowled, uttered a canine whine of his own. Yet again, he formed a fist in the air.

"CRUSH HEAD!"

***

A little ways down from where the dog now lay dead—its head crushed into a softball-sized sphere of compacted flesh, mashed brains, shattered bone, and bloody fur—a blue garbage truck rounded the corner of an intersecting side street and pulled alongside the curb, where two wheeled trashed bins stood on a tree lawn. Two black garbagemen—Cedric and DeAndre by name—stepped off the side of the truck. When a garbage load on a tree lawn consisted of just a few trash bins, DeAndre, who was sixteen years younger than 50-year-old Cedric, often did the lifting and dumping while the older man operated the compacter.

As DeAndre went to grab the first trash bin, Cedric leaned up against the side of the truck and extracted a cigarette and a box of matches from the front pocket of his shirt. Just as he shook the burning match out after he lit the cig, he glanced up to see the propeller beanie man turning onto the apron of the driveway to approach him. He halted about two arms' length away from Cedric.

"Are you the girl with ribbons in her hair?" the propeller beanie man asked.

Cedric jerked his head back, scoffing as he flicked the extinguished match away. "Say what?"

"Are you the girl with ribbons in her hair?"

Cedric pushed himself off the side of the truck, puffed his chest out a bit. "The fuck you talkin' about?"

"Are you the girl with ribbons in her hair?"

"Pfft!" Cedric turned to DeAndre, who had stopped to observe the exchange; he stood holding a trash bin in his gloved hands, one eyebrow arched as he cast a quizzical look at the propeller beanie man. Locking eyes with his coworker, Cedric jabbed a thumb at the propeller beanie man. "The hell he talkin' about?"

"Are you the girl with ribbons in her hair?" the propeller beanie man asked.

Cedric turned back to face him, leaned in close, the two men's noses nearly touching. "Muthafucka, do I look like a girl with ribbons in her hair?" he asked through clenched teeth.

"Are you the girl with ribbons in her hair?"

Cedric shook his head in dismay. "I suggest you keep walkin', big man. We tryin' to work here."

"Are you the girl with ribbons in her hair?"

"That's it! Get the fuck outta here, ya weird-ass muthafucka," Cedric said. He went to shove the propeller beanie man, intending to send him stumbling backwards. But just before the garbageman's open palms came into contact with the propeller beanie man's chest, they exploded.

Shrieking, Cedric stared wide-eyed at his maimed forearms, blood jetting out in long, rhythmic spurts from his ragged wrist stumps in time with his heartbeat.

"Muuuthafucka!" DeAndre said, slack jawed as he let the garbage bin fall to the lawn.

"CRUSH HEAD!" the propeller beanie man said, making a fist. Cedric's cheekbones sunk in as his jaw pushed up into his skull, his forehead swallowing his horror-stricken eyeballs as his eye sockets collapsed in on themselves, the bones of his head cracking audibly as they caved in around his brain.

Felipe, the driver of the garbage truck, climbed down from the cabin to see what was going on. Close in age to Cedric, the Hispanic man halted beside DeAndre. "What in the blue fuck?" he uttered, terror-stricken, just as Cedric's handless and mostly headless body toppled to the curb.

The front of his homemade "I LOVE MY MOM AND MY GRANDPAPS" t-shirt now stained bright crimson with the dead garbageman's blood, the propeller beanie man turned and pointed at Felipe. "Are *you* the girl with ribbons in her hair?"

Slowly backpedaling away from the gruesome scene, Felipe turned tail and ran for it.

He didn't get far.

"CRUSH HEAD!"

The propeller beanie man turned to DeAndre, who, paralyzed with fear, had not moved from where he'd dropped the garbage bin on the tree lawn. The man pointed at him. "Are *you* the girl with ribbons in her hair?"

DeAndre didn't hesitate. He nodded his head rapidly, held his palms out in the air in a gesture of submission. "Yeah, man. I'm the girl with ribbons in her hair. That's me!"

The propeller beanie man let out a high-pitched whine, but this time one of excitement. He briskly clapped his hands together in front of his face. "Oh, goody! I'm so glad I finally found you!"

As he moved closer to DeAndre, the propeller beanie man reached into a fanny pack mostly hidden beneath his prodigious gut, unzipped it, and pulled out a yellow wig styled in pigtails tied with pink ribbons. He carefully fitted the wig atop DeAndre's head.

"Hey, maybe there's another girl with ribbons in her hair around here," he said. "Let's go see!"

DeAndre gulped dryly. "Whatever you say, homie."

***

Near the end of his morning jog, Myles glanced down at his wrist pedometer: 3.2 miles so far. If he turned left down Sylvania—the next side street—rounded the block, and took Ridge all the way back home, that would put him at about his desired four miles.

As he turned onto Sylvania, he saw a cluster of three people a few driveways ahead of him. One of the people was a tall, pale-faced, overweight man wearing a propeller beanie and a mostly red shirt. Next to him stood a black man garbed in the work gloves, pants, and reflective yellow shirt of an outdoor manual laborer, but also wearing a yellow wig with pigtails tied in ribbons.

Weird, Myles couldn't help but think. The propeller beanie man and the wigged man faced Myles' direction. These two men appeared to be conversing with the third person—a short, older woman dressed for yardwork, her long, frizzy gray hair pulled back in a loose ponytail. Her back to Myles, the woman wore yard gloves and gripped a handheld weeder in one hand.

Myles kept up his pace. After he passed the first driveway, he moved over to a tree lawn so that he could pass the people on the sidewalk. He glanced over to see the woman shaking her head in response to something said to her. That's when he noticed the propeller beanie man's red shirt gleamed wetly in the morning sun, as if the shirt were wet with...

The propeller beanie man raised a claw-bent hand into the air and clutched his fingers together into a fist.

By then, Myles was near enough to hear the sick cracking of bone and popping of ligament as the woman's head broke apart, hot blood and brains running down the back of her shirt.

Myles stopped dead in his tracks, not twenty feet away from where the woman collapsed dead onto her back. Struggling to catch his breath, he stared down at the body, dumbstruck, as the propeller beanie man and the wigged man approached him. He looked up from the corpse, glanced from one man to the other.

"What the hell just happened to her?" Myles blurted.

"Are you the girl with ribbons in her hair?" the propeller beanie guy asked, pointing at him.

"Whuh-whuh-what?"

"I'd strongly advise you to say *yes*," the wigged man said, an expression of deep concern on his face. He half-turned in place to jab a thumb back at the corpse. "I tried to tell the lady there, but she wouldn't listen. She said no. That's what happens when you say no to him. Big man here has some fucked up supernatural powers you don't wanna fuck with. If you don't say yes to him, you end up like her."

The propeller beanie man continued to point at Myles, as if in condemnation. "Are you the girl with ribbons in her hair?"

Myles glanced from the propeller beanie man's face to the wigged man's face, then back to the propeller beanie man.

"Um, yeah. That's me. I'm the girl with ribbons in her hair."

A shrill whine of excitement escaped the propeller beanie man's throat as he clapped his hands together before his face. "Oh, swell! Now there's two of you!"

He extracted another yellow wig, one identical to the wig on the garbageman's head, from his fanny pack and fitted it onto the jogger's head.

"I think it's time for you two to meet Mother!"

***

Following the trail of corpses he'd made that morning, the propeller beanie man retraced his steps through the neighborhood and led Myles and DeAndre back to a rusty 1970, white Ford van, sitting in the parking lot of a local park. Written on the driver's side of the van, a tad more legibly than on the propeller beanie man's t-shirt were the words "I LOVE MY MOM AND MY GRANDPAPS" in streaky, maroon paint. After ordering his captives into the back of the van and slamming the door on them, the propeller beanie man went around to the driver's seat, climbed in, and they were off.

They drove on a state highway for nearly forty minutes, before getting off at an exit somewhere in the boonies. The van followed a country road that snaked and rolled through alternating stretches of wooded hills, crop fields, and pastures. At some point the van slowed down to turn onto a narrow unmarked, gravel road that took them deeper into the wooded countryside. Minutes later, the road opened up onto a dead-end clearing where stood an old, ramshackle Victorian farmhouse rising out of a lush sea of knee-high, breeze-tousled grass dotted with spring wildflowers.

Painted in black block letters across the colorless, sun-bleached surface of the house's largest gable were the words "I LOVE MY MOM AND MY GRANDPAPS."

***

Waiting for the propeller beanie man to return from the basement, their doll-like wigs still in place, DeAndre and Myles found themselves ensconced in two musty, old high-back chairs in the unlit sitting room of the farmhouse, a coffee table separating them from a couch positioned against the wall. Their eyes were still adjusting to the relative darkness of the room, an inadequate illumination that was done by design; boards and heavy drapes covered all the windows, letting in only a few thin shafts of filtered sunlight here and there. But the captives couldn't help but notice how another darkness, one blacker than the ambient gloom that engulfed the rest of the room, gathered around the couch across from them, as if through some unnatural phenomenon that prevented the ambient light from reaching that part of the room. Within that deeper darkness, a barely discernible, vaguely human-like shape sat on the couch, still as death. Two tiny pinpoints of gray light glowed faintly in the figure's elongated gourd-like head, nearly imperceptible and set much lower in the face than a normal human's eyes.

The propeller beanie man emerged from the dark behind them to stand between the two chairs. "Sorry to keep you all waiting. I had to check on Grandpaps. Mother, these are the girls with ribbons in their hair. Girls with ribbons in their hair, this is Mother."

The Möthęr-Thǐng slowly leaned forward on the couch, as if to get a better look at the two guests, her misshapen head tilting to one side. Though she was still mostly hidden in the unnatural darkness enshrouding the couch, DeAndre and Myles saw her a little more clearly now, the form of her body revealing gray-hued hints of incongruous textures: a round spot of what appeared to be loose, wrinkled skin melding into a patch of something that resembled smooth plaster. Something like a wet rag set alongside what might be tangles of rusty wire. An ovular patch of what appeared to be coarse animal hair, bordered on one side by shards of broken glass arranged in a crude mosaic pattern.

The Möthẹr-Thǐng emitted an unintelligible, low-pitched whisper, that, after a moment, modulated into a higher-pitched hiss interspersed with short bursts of mechanical, alien-sounding clicks.

"Mother said you two are very pretty," the propeller beanie man said.

DeAndre and Myles remained silent, though they turned to each other and exchanged wide-eyed looks of abject terror.

"Where are your manners? Tell Mother, 'thank you.'"

"Thank you," the captives said in muted chorus.

The propeller beanie man took a step closer to the Mȯthẹr-Thĭng. "I'm going to ask them to marry me now, Mother!"

The Mȯthẹr-Thĭng vocalized another susurrus mixed with more snakelike hissing and bursts of insectile clicks. This communication was slightly louder and more agitated than her previous one.

The propeller beanie man whimpered. "Oh, no! Mother says I'm a bad man for wanting to marry both of you. She says it would be indecent, heathenish, and sinful for me to have two wives."

The Mȯthẹr-Thĭng uttered more nightmarish noise.

"Okay, Mother. I'll choose one."

The propeller beanie man moved in front of the men to see them better. Stroking his pimply chin in contemplation, he glanced back and forth from one man's face to the other for a good ten minutes before he finally knelt down on one knee to face Myles. He grasped one of the man's limp hands in his own."

"The girl with ribbons in her hair, w-w-will you m-m-m-m-m-m-m-marry m-m-m-me?"

A lone tear of despair escaped Myles' eye as he looked to DeAndre, as if for help. All DeAndre could do for the luckless man was offer him an eyeful of sympathy before a pang of survivor guilt forced him to avert his eyes to the floor. Myles then turned away from DeAndre, let his head drop into his hands. "Yes," he said in a near-whisper.

"Oh, swell!" the propeller beanie man said, patting his own face repeatedly with the pads of his fingers.

"Um, does that mean...I can, like, go now?" DeAndre asked.

The Möthęr-Thǐng expelled more terrible sounds.

"Yes. Mother said you are free to go."

DeAndre slowly rose from his chair, afraid that a sudden movement might call attention to himself and possibly make the propeller beanie man and the Möthęr-Thǐng reconsider his release. He removed the wig from his head, gingerly set it on the chair and took one last look around the room. At the doomed, wigged man holding his face in his hands. At the propeller beanie man whose smiling, maniacal visage hung in the darkness, like a disembodied phantom head, and at the Möthęr-Thǐng's pinpoint eyes—like dying ash-colored stars—staring at him from within that unaccountable gathering of darkness.

He turned around and shuffled towards a dimly lit rectangle that marked the threshold of the hallway, through which the propeller beanie man had led them into the sitting room earlier. Following the corridor to the front entrance of the house, DeAndre's pace quickened the further away from the sitting room he got. He did not slow down as he passed the open passageway to the basement staircase, from which emanated the whistling wheezes and low moans of the Grândpā-Thïng stirring around down there in the dark.

After DeAndre exited the house via the front door and crossed the sunken porch, he launched into a sprint, as if the devil himself were hot on his heels. He fled the clearing, following the gravel road back the way they'd come.

He got about a quarter mile away from the house when he realized he'd forgotten to do something important back there. Breathing heavily, he stopped in his tracks, did an about-face, and started jogging back.

When he arrived back at the front porch, he paused to catch his breath, leaning forward and resting his hands on his knees. He then knocked four times on the top of the screen door. A beat later, the front door pulled inward with a creak, to reveal the propeller beanie man framed in the interior gloom beyond the screen.

"My man," DeAndre said, smiling and holding up a hand in greeting.

"What do you want?"

"Hey, I know you chose that other dude to marry instead of me—believe me, I'm cool with that, yo. But I was just wonderin': would you mind choppin' my arms and legs off with a chainsaw, cauterizin' the stumps with a blowtorch, gougin' out both my eyes, cuttin' out my tongue, fuckin' up my eardrums with somethin' sharp— like an icepick maybe—then chainin' what's left of me up to the wall down in the basement here?"

The propeller beanie man stared at him, frowning.

"You could feed me a bit of food n' water every day," DeAndre resumed. "I wouldn't need much food. Just enough to keep me alive. Shit, I eat dog food if that's all y'all can afford. I want y'all to let me live down there in the basement as your deaf, dumb, blind, quadruple amputee prisoner for the rest of my days."

The propeller beanie man clutched at his own face with one hand for a moment, anxiously kneading his chubby cheeks so hard that it hurt him as he considered DeAndre's request.

"I'll have to go ask Mother if that would be alright." He turned away, disappeared into the gloom of the house.

DeAndre put an ear up to the screen, listened to the sound of the obese man's creaky, heavy footsteps receding down the hallway. The footfalls stopped moments later, their sound replaced by the propeller beanie man's hushed speech followed by the Möthęr-Thïng's sibilant whispers and hellish clicks, all of which DeAndre heard quite well owing to the acoustics of the house's bare hardwood flooring, combined with the relative emptiness of the place. He could even hear the faint moaning and wheezing of the Grândpā-Thïng down in the basement.

After a time, the footsteps took up again, starting off softly, each new one falling slightly louder than the one before it, before the propeller beanie man reemerged from the darkness.

"Mother said she'll grant you your request."

DeAndre pumped both his fists out before him. "Aw, hells yeah!"

"But under one condition."

DeAndre's hands fell to his sides. "What's that?"

"Before we chop your arms and legs off and stuff, Mother insists that you make love to her. See, she's never made love to a black man before, and she's always wanted to."

DeAndre grinned big. "Heh. Oh, that's no problem at all. I'll take real good care of your moms, if that's what she wants."

"But you need my approval, too. What are you gonna do for me if I agree to let you live as a deaf, dumb, blind, quadruple amputee prisoner in my basement?"

"What'll I do for you? Shit, muthafucka—I do anything. You want me to suck yo dick? Then I suck yo dick, see? You want me to suck the shit outta yo big, white honky ass? Then I suck the shit outta yo big, white honky ass. Like I said, nigga, I'll do anything to live down there in your muthafuckin' basement, all deaf, dumb, and blind n' shit!"

The propeller beanie man pushed the screen door open, and DeAndre backed up to give him room as he stepped out onto the porch.

"My mom chopped off my dick many years ago when she caught me touching myself behind the barn. She still has it, keeps it in a cigar box under her bed. So, you sucking my dick wouldn't do me a whole lotta good these days. And I'm not really interested in you eating shit out of my ass."

"A'ight, my man. Then what you want?"

"I...I want you to marry my Grandpaps. So that...so that you'll be my grandma. Considering Grandpaps already lives in the basement, it'll be a convenient union for the two of you." A tear then sprung to his eye. "I...I've always wanted to have a deaf, dumb, blind, quadruple amputee, black man as a grandma."

DeAndre's eyes teared up as well. "But are you sure yo granddaddy want a deaf, dumb, blind, quadruple amputee, black man as a wife?"

"He's not very picky about stuff."

DeAndre shook his head as if in disbelief at his good fortune. He opened his arms wide. "Gimme a hug, my tiny little grandson!"

Grandmother and grandson then embraced for the first time.

And no one lived happily ever after (including no one in real life).

The End

Soft White Underbelly

By

Tim Curran

Nicky Spiro had a hard-on about the whole thing.

His dark eyes were blazing like cutting torches and everyone was cringing from the heat. He tapped one long, skeletal finger to his cheekbone, saying, "This fuck is way out of bounds. He wants money? I give him money. He wants time? I give him time. But now he's making a fool out of me, you understand that? He treats me like—" he symbolically spit on the carpeting "—like shit, like something you step in and wipe off your shoe. You boys understand that? You understand what I'm saying about this? You understand why the freak has to go?"

They did.

There were three of them seated in the office of Nick the Greek's Lafayette Street restaurant, Little Athens: Johnny Six, Frank Vagris, and Petros "Fat Pete" Skolakis. They sat side by side on the sofa like a trio of delinquents hauled in before the principal. Johnny Six was long and lean, dark like a Mediterranean night; Frank was short, fair, stocky as a burning barrel, and Fat Pete at six-feet-seven, 350 pounds, was just everywhere big.

Frank said, "We been over there twice this fucking month, Nick, ain't we? The last time we went in there, we started breaking up the place."

Johnny Six nodded. "We busted-up his cash register, broke his windows, shattered his fucking display cases. We trashed the place. The other day—I drive by there and you know what? You know what? Windows are fixed, people going in and out. What the fuck is with this goob? We gotta break legs and shit?"

Nicky pulled a cigarette out of the case on his desk, showed it some flame. He looked to Frank because Frank was the smart one. "Tell me about the freak. What kind of shit is he into?"

Frank shrugged. "He makes up cures, you know? You go in there with bad knees or a soft pecker and he mixes up some crushed bugs and leaves and what not, brews it for you. Like medicine. Just like I told you before."

"Fucking witch doctor," Johnny Six said.

Fat Pete hadn't said a thing. You wanted a door broken down? You wanted someone's head opened with a pipe? Fat Pete was your guy. But when he spoke, it became real apparent his head was empty as a shoebox. He was good muscle and nothing more. He didn't have the brainpower to light a refrigerator bulb.

Nicky sucked off his cigarette. "Well, fuck it, I'm sick of this guy. You boys go over there and do what I tell you. Burn him. Plant him. I want this fuck over with."

Frank nodded. "Anything special?"

Nicky just stared at him. "Do it clean. Make him a fucking ghost."

***

The freak's name was Gribbens.

He was a dwarfish man with oily skin just as brown as smoked fish, hunched and twisted as if some tremendous weight pressed down upon him. He'd spent his life as a sideshow entertainer in New York and Chicago and was considered to be something of a legendary escape artist and contortionist. Rumor had it he could withstand punishments that would kill lesser men. That, as part of his act, he'd been hung, stabbed, electrocuted. Steamrollers had driven over him and draft horses had tried to pull him apart. It was said he'd lived for three days frozen solid in ice, was kept for a month in a glass case of highly-venomous scorpions, had spent a fortnight in a snakepit of deadly black mambas and had been bitten repeatedly, but did not die. His greatest accomplishment (it was claimed) was being submerged in New York's East River in a chained casket for five days.

He was the son of sideshow performers and had spent his formative years in India and the Orient. Five years ago he showed up in Detroit's Greektown wanting to open some sort of natural pharmacy. Nicky had rented him a building, loaned him the money to get going. He hung out his shingle and started selling herbs and roots and dried insects and mummified animal parts, holistic medicines. Most of his customers were Arabs and Asians. He was supposed to be good at curing ills and ailments, but wasn't much of a businessman. Gave too much credit and wasn't inclined to collect.

Not that any of that bullshit mattered to Nicky Spiro. He wanted his rent and wanted the vig on the original loan. Twenty-grand with ten percent interest rolled over weekly, $2000. Thing was, Gribbens had yet to touch the principal (which was okay) and had not met the vig in over six months (not okay).

Intimidation and gentle persuasion had borne no fruit.

Now it was time for Nicky to cut his losses.

Gribbens was going to die.

***

The sign above the door read: APOTHECARY.

It was barely legible, faded gray like cigarette ash. Frank Vagris, Fat Pete, and Johnny Six entered the store and wrinkled their noses at the powdery, peppery smells that filled the place like an Egyptian tomb. They wore black rain slickers and leather gloves. They made their way to the back past the feathers and bones and jars of dehydrated spiders and lizards. The display cases had all been repaired now. Apparently the freak had the money to do that, but not to pay his bills. They found him in his office.

"Gentlemen," he said, nodding to them, his eyes like blanched olives floating in greasy swill. "I knew you would come, sooner or later."

Frank said, "Six months now. We've been real easy on you, you know that, don't you?"

Gribbens rose from behind the card table he used as a desk, closed the cover of an old book that looked like it was bound in skin. "I appreciate your patience. The patience of Mister Nick. But I am a poor man—"

"Like we give a fuck," Johnny Six said. "You borrowed the money, you don't pay the interest. Way we see it, you're not going to."

Gribbens studied the rain slickers they wore, the gloves. He knew very well it wasn't raining out. He smiled thinly. "A moment, perhaps, to confer with my god."

Johnny Six said, "Sure, no problem, asshole."

Before the words had left his mouth, both Frank and he took out silenced .45 auto handguns and, without further ado, started emptying them into him. Still smiling, the bullets ripped into him and he jumped like a mouse on a hotplate, blood and tissue raining against the wall behind him. When he finally went down, the air choked with smoke and blood-mist, his body had more holes in it than a cheese grater.

Fat Pete went to grab the sheets out of the van, but Johnny Six stopped him.

"Hey," he said. "What the fuck is this?"

Leaning up against the far wall was a wooden crate discolored with water stains. Frank and Johnny Six

101

popped the lid. There was a skeleton inside. An old one, the bones gone yellow and pitted with worm holes.

"What the fuck was this guy into?" Frank said.

They dumped the bones out and dropped Gribbens into it, nailed the lid down. They loaded the box in the van. When that was done, they poured gas all over the store and tossed a road flare in through the doorway. The building went up like napalm. Nicky wanted it that way. He'd collect the insurance, raze the building, and put up something that would make money.

Frank and the others drove north out of Detroit, past Mechanic City, towards Mount Clemens, found a dirt county road and planted the box about a hundred yards into the trees, in a five-foot hole.

And that was it.

**

A few days later, Nicky Spiro had a bash in one of the private dining rooms at Little Athens. Everyone was there. The entire crew. The room was filled with hookers and gamblers, cops and politicians on the take, street soldiers and racketeers. The criminal underbelly of the motor city was exposed. There was talent from Chicago. Players from Milwaukee, Cleveland, Kansas City, even a couple greasers from New York. There was a fine selection of Cypriot wines and Greek beer. The buffet tables were overflowing with seafood and Greek culinary delights—moussaka, lamb chops, exohiko, pastitsio, puddings, soups, breads. There was music and dancing and laughter.

Johnny Six was telling jokes like usual. But there was something bothering him. Frank could see that much. He kept taking off into the bathroom, holding his belly. So Frank followed him in there.

"What's a matter?" he asked.

Johnny Six was puking into the toilet. When he finished he wiped his mouth with toilet paper. "I don't know. I gotta fucking bug or something. I can't keep nothing down." Frank helped him up off his knees, steered him towards the sinks. Johnny Six stared at his reflection, splashed water in his face. "Puking all the time. All day long. I mean, I don't feel bad. I just can't keep nothing down. And my skin—Jesus, I'm so fucking itchy I think I got the lice or something."

Frank told him to go home and lay down. Left him scratching furiously at his back like a hound working a tick.

Somewhere during the festivities, Nicky pulled Frank aside, kissed him on both cheeks and poured him a glass of fifty-year old Athiri. "That thing the other day," he said into his ear. "You know that thing, Frank? The one I talk about?"

"Sure, Nick. I know."

"You handled that fine, just fine. But we don't talk no more about that, right?"

"Not a word."

Nicky studied him, a strategist looking for an opening. Frank gave him none; he knew Nicky too well.

Nicky had a psychotic temper if he thought you were playing him or fucking him behind his back. One time, a pizza boy forgot the black olives on his deep dish and Nicky started screaming obscenities at him, pulled out a .38 snub-nose and put three rounds into him. He was real sweet like that.

"That guy. That freak. You remember his name?" he asked pointedly.

"What guy?" Frank said. "What freak?"

Nicky hugged him. "You a good boy, Frank."

***

Three days later, Johnny Six dropped out of sight.

He was the sort of guy who was always around, always hungry for a piece of this, a piece of that. He had a pretty good loansharking business going, a lot of money on the streets. But even his runners hadn't seen him. In fact, no one had seen him since the party the other night.

Frank and Johnny Six had grown up together, worked the streets together, had done a stretch of state time in the same cell. They were closer than spoons in a drawer. And when he went missing for three days running, Frank knew there was trouble.

Johnny Six lived in a four-story walk-up tenement that hailed from the days before the First World War. It was a dingy, ugly slab of brick that was like an oven in the summer and an icebox in the winter. He lived on the top floor. Place was peopled mostly by immigrants—Greeks, Russians, assorted Slavs. It had no elevator and smelled of age, sweat, and fried foods flavored by cat piss. Johnny Six could have lived better, easy, but he claimed he liked the atmosphere.

By the time Frank reached the fourth floor, he could smell something sour, something unpleasant. Some little woman with a scarf over her head was peering out her door. She motioned towards Johnny Six's place, crossed herself and babbled in a foreign tongue.

Frank ignored her, hammered on Johnny Six's door.

Nothing.

He could hear something in there, a gurgling wet sound like a backed-up toilet. Nothing else. It was as quiet as a morgue. He knocked again, then pressed his hand flat against the door. It felt warm. Oddly warm for an October night.

"Johnny?" he called out. "You in there?"

A voice said, "Go the fuck away."

Frank felt something cold spread over his skin. Jesus, that voice. It didn't even sound like Johnny Six. It sounded mushy, congested, like he was speaking with a mouthful of wet leaves.

Frank tried the doorknob. It was open. He pushed it in an inch, two, three. The stink hit him right away: flyblown and putrid like somebody had been taking core samples from a mass grave. It made him step back. The air was thick with it, hot and steaming.

"Johnny, it's Frank."

The voice came again: "Frank?" he said, like maybe he had to think on it a bit, remember who this Frank was. "What do you want here? You better just go."

"You sick?"

"Yeah."

There were no lights on in there, just a bit of illumination from the street trying to poke its way around drawn shades. Frank stepped in, sucked breath through clenched teeth. The air was humid and heavy, like trying to inhale swamp gas.

He knew his way around the place by feel. He found a chair up against the wall, directly across from what he assumed was Johnny Six, an odd, black shape lounged on the couch. There was something about that shape— something disturbing. There was a space heater in the corner going full blast. It was well over a hundred degrees in the apartment.

"Why don't you let me get you to a doctor?" Frank said to him.

"Too late for that. Just get out, okay?" he made strange, strangled weeping sounds. "Get out. I can't think straight no more, Frank. I don't know who I am."

Frank swallowed down a mouthful of sand. "What do you mean, Johnny?"

"I don't know...it's like...like somebody's in my head."

"For fuck's sake, Johnny, that don't make no sense."

Frank had to fight with himself not to gag. His nose was filled with that stagnant putrescence and he badly wanted to vomit. But more than that, he wanted to run far away. But Johnny Six was his friend. Abandoning him at his time of need was unthinkable. It wasn't in Frank's make-up. But that stink, Christ, it was all over him. Like being splashed with a bucket of rotting entrails. A high, hot smell of bacterial decay.

Frank's fingers danced in his shirt pocket, found cigarettes. Trembling, he put one in his mouth, lit it. And in the momentary glow from the lighter, he caught a glimpse of Johnny Six. Not much of one, but enough to fuel dozens of nightmares. He was wrapped up in a blanket, bloated and distorted like he'd been filled with helium and was slowly deflating. He seemed oddly boneless like maybe it was only the blanket that held him together, kept him from spilling all over the floor. He was all wet and glistening.

The cigarette fell from Frank's lips. "Johnny...Jesus Christ, this is fucking bullshit, man. I'm turning on the lights."

"No," the voice warned. "You don't wanna do that."

So Frank didn't.

He honestly didn't want to know or see anymore. It was enough. By God, it was enough. His flesh crawling, he made his way to the door, shaking all over like a kid trying to fight his way out of a carnival spook house. There was a sound behind him like wet cement poured into a pail. He realized then that Johnny Six was sitting up, maybe trying to find his feet.

With a cry, Frank threw the door open and Johnny Six make a weird squealing sound as the hallway light hit him. Frank looked and wished he hadn't. Because the blanket had fallen off and he got a good look at Johnny Six. And that was bad enough, but what really made him run out of there was what was opening in Johnny Six's skin.

Eyes. Dozens of watery, yellow eyes.

***

Tony Pojis was Nicky Spiro's underboss. He was the guy who handled all the day-to-day operations like a sort of criminal office manager. But unlike Nicky who was vulgar and street-wise and menacing, Pojis was a soft-spoken man. Intelligent, educated, he had a knack for making money like any good businessman.

After Frank had swallowed half a bottle of brandy and told his tale, Pojis just sat there in his recliner, gently rocking and rocking.

"And what do you think?" he said in all sincerity. "What do you think happened to him?"

Frank had a few ideas. But he didn't dare speak them. Before he could stop himself, though, they fell out of his mouth. "It's that guy, the one..." He paused, knowing that after a guy was whacked, he no longer existed. You were not allowed to mention him. "I don't know...I keep thinking about the freak."

Pojis stroked his thick black mustache. "You think he had something to do with this?"

"I guess. I don't know."

"But he's dead."

"Yeah. I know."

Pojis thought about it some more, sipped some brandy. Frank knew if it was anyone else, they would have laughed at him and thrown his ass out the door. But Pojis wasn't like that. You could trust him to always say and do the right thing.

Finally, he licked his lips, said, "You believe in magic, Frank?"

"Course not."

"Witchcraft?"

"Fuck no."

Pojis sighed, rolled a cigar in his lips, but did not light it. "You never knew my mother, eh, Frank? No, gone these past twenty years. God bless her. Boy, she was some kind of woman, all right." He laughed out loud, mouth open, his mustache looking like a spider crawling out of a hole. "You know why I never got married? I'll tell you. It's because I could never find a woman that was half the broad my mother was. But why am I telling you about my mother?"

Frank just shrugged. A guy like Pojis wanted to spin tales about his dear old mother, then why not? He could do whatever he wanted.

"I tell you because my mother told me a story once. A story I want you should hear. So just bear with me, okay?" Pojis set the cigar down, started stroking his mustache again. His eyes twinkled blue with memories of his mother, then went dark like a stormy sky. "My mother was from a little village in Cyprus called Volgis. Just a little farming village at the foot of Mount Troodos. Wine country. When she was a little girl these two criminals came to town, she said. The Kovoros bothers. They were bandits and killers. Using violence and intimidation, they quickly took over the vineyards, they and their hoods. They made Volgis a bad place to live. Men were gunned down in the streets, farmers beaten, girls raped. Even the local police were in their pockets. Nothing could be done. Well, eventually people could take no more. A group of village elders met secretly and decided they would make the pilgrimage up the mountain to see the old lady they called Mama Koda. She was a witch and everyone feared her. It was said Mama Koda could blight crops or call down the moon, cure the sick and raise the dead.

"So, they went up there and Mama Koda told them, for a price, she could help them. Her price? Nothing extravagant, just a monthly delivery of food and wine be brought to her. She was getting old—nobody dared guess how old, but my mother said maybe old as the mountain—and couldn't get around so well.

"Anyway, a week passes, nothing. Two weeks, nothing. People begin to ridicule the village elders and their pagan ways. But then something does happen, you see. The two Kovoros brothers are found one morning screaming in their beds. My mother was one of those who saw them, saw the horrible thing that had happened to them. You see, a doctor was fetched from a nearby village because even the wisest of the elders could not believe what they were seeing. The Kovoros brothers had been reduced to blobs. Like jellyfish, my mother said. They could not move, could barely breath and speak. They died that night. The doctor performed an autopsy. And you know what, Frank? Neither of the Kovoros brothers had any bones in them. Their skeletons...just gone."

Frank sat there, studying his feet. He had so much weird shit tangled in his brain by that point, he didn't really doubt any of it. He didn't know what to say, so he said nothing.

Pojis toyed with his cigar. "You probably think this is some folk-tale imported from the old country to frighten the kids into being good boys and girls." He shrugged. "Maybe it is. All I can say is that my mother swore it was true. And I believe her. She was a tough, practical, unimaginative sort of woman, Frank. She didn't go for ghost stories. And why do I tell you this? I tell you because I believe certain people have talents beyond that which you and I know or can guess of. Talents, ancient knowledge, whatever. You could call these talents witchcraft or black magic. Call it whatever you want."

Frank felt like the blood was evaporating from his veins. He felt dry and ready to crumble. "And you think the freak was one of them?"

Pojis did. And gave as evidence the sort of store he operated, the things he was claimed to have done. His unbelievable history with the sideshows.

"You think a normal man can live through those things?"

Frank just shook his head. "I don't know what to think."

"What I'm getting at, Frank, is that the freak might be avenging himself. Crazy as that sounds."

Revenge from beyond the grave. That kind of shit belonged on the late show. Or maybe in the far, dim past in the old country. But not now. Not here in Detroit.

"So what do we do?" Frank said, lighting a cigarette.

Pojis shrugged. "Maybe nothing, maybe everything. First we gather facts. That's all we can do."

"Where do we start?"

"You weren't on that job alone. It was you and Johnny Six and Fat Pete."

Frank's eyes got wide like rising moons. "Fat Pete. I haven't seen him around."

Pojis nodded. "And neither has anyone else."

***

Frank mounted the stairs and it took all the strength he had. Fat Pete lived in his mother's old house in Royal Oak. And this is where Frank was now. The house was quiet, incredibly still as if it was holding its breath.

"Pete?" Frank called out, knowing it was pretty useless by that point. His voice echoed and died in the gravelike silence. He'd been all through the house calling for Pete and the entire time he knew where he had to go:

117

up the stairs. But it wasn't until he heard the floorboards above creak that he forced himself up there. "Pete? You around? It's Frank. I gotta talk to you."

No response.

Just the house lying about him huge and still and brooding, as if deep in its black, vacant heart it held a dark and terrible secret. Frank kept going up, listening to cars passing, out on the street, kids playing in the yard next door. It all seemed so positively ordinary that the terror in his heart was all that much worse. Things like this couldn't happen here, not in the heart of an industrialized Midwestern city.

"Pete?" he called again, not as loudly now, maybe afraid that someone would hear. "Pete?"

He could smell a stink up there. A raw, festering smell like a dead cat boiling with worms. It turned something in him to sauce.

And part of him, that street-wise tough guy, wanted to laugh at it all. He'd been in gangs and prison fights, he'd murdered men and beaten others nearly to death. His had been a tight, violent world where only the most vicious predators stayed alive. But here he was, ready to piss himself, ready to—

Someone was standing at the top of the stairs.

Frank nearly screamed.

It was Fat Pete—but it wasn't Fat Pete. A big and hulking form limned with shadow, a swollen face the color of oatmeal and roughly the same texture. The eyes stared unblinking down at him, totally devoid of anything human. Drool ran from the corners of the lips. Teeth were bared and there was a deranged hissing sound deep in the throat.

Frank said, "Pete?"

The form stood there and then turned away suddenly with odd, jerking motions. It was an almost comical walk, like a puppet manipulated by strings, a loose-limbed, see-sawing shamble.

Frank watched him, rooted to the spot like an old oak.

Pete was dressed in a bathrobe—he used to joke that a tent-maker made his clothes for him—and the funny thing, the real frightening thing, was that it looked like Pete had a hiker's backpack or rucksack under the robe at his shoulders. There was a huge, grotesque bulge there that seemed to twitch as he walked.

Frank nearly fell down the stairs getting out of there.

In his car, trembling, his mind filled with noise, a soothing voice told him it couldn't get any worse.

But it was dead wrong.

***

The next night they opened the freak's grave.

It was just the two of them—Frank and Pojis. They came with shovels and guns and an ugly, unspeakable feeling in the pits of their bellies. They didn't speak much on the drive up. And when they did it was about anything but what was on their minds.

Pojis pulled his Lincoln into the trees, the hi-beams casting wild, lurching shadows everywhere. The woods, so dark and murky, pressed in from all sides, witnesses to something dark and ancient. The wind was blowing, a mist in the air.

It was bad.

Frank brushed dead leaves from the grave. Then, together, they started to dig.

The sound of shovels biting into the damp, rich earth was like some distant thunder that echoed through their brains. The soil was black and clotted, moist and wormy.

Frank kept his mind blank, emptied it like a cup, because that was the only way to hang onto his sanity. Just keep shoveling, keep digging, think of nothing but the spade eating into the earth, deeper and deeper. Focus, that's what. Don't think of what you're doing or even what you expect to find, because you do, you do and—

The wind cried with a mournful noise in the treetops. They could hear crackling sounds out in the forest as if something was circling, getting closer and

121

closer. And the worst thing, the very worst thing, was the inexplicable, utterly dreadful feeling of being watched. Neither of them could shake it. That sensation of cold, remorseless eyes on them.

Thud.

Frank struck wood.

Pojis climbed out of the grave and gave him room. He trained a flashlight down there. Using a crowbar, Frank popped the nails free. Sucking in dry, rattling breaths, he slid his fingers under the lid and opened it, his heart pounding like a voodoo drum.

The freak's clothes had gone brown with old blood, numerous holes drilled into the body. His face was a death mask. The coffin was filled with something pooling and shifting, something viscid and sentient and hideously alive.

"Oh, Christ," Frank said, feeling whatever it was crawling over his flesh and settling into him in a black malignance.

Gribbens' eyes were open, filled with a baleful hatred that made Frank's skin go tight. They were yellow and glistening like the ones set into Johnny Six's body.

One of his brown, shriveled arms fell from his belly, the knuckles rapping on the side of the box. And his lips, they spread slowly and inexorably into a ghastly, hungry grin.

Frank barely got out of there.

But he did, pushing Pojis aside, grabbing a twelve-gauge Remington sawed-off just above the pump. He aimed it into the grave, shrieking: "You don't wanna die, motherfucker? You wanna live forever you goddamn freak, you goddamn witch, you fucking piece of shit—"

And all the while, he was squeezing off rounds. Blowing holes in what laid in the box until there was nothing left but rags and flaps of flesh like confetti dropped at a parade.

Until Pojis said, "Enough, Frank. Enough."

After that, they poured kerosene in the box and burned everything in there to ash, silently staring as greasy plumes of smoke rose from the burning pit. When that was done, they filled in the grave and drove away in silence.

***

Frank disappeared for a few days after that one.

Nothing weird happened to him, he just started drinking. In fact, once he started it took him two days of concentrated boozing to get the sight of the freak out of his mind. But eventually, he came back.

And when he did, Pojis was waiting for him.

"Where the hell you been?" he said, uncharacteristically pissed. "You don't just walk away from this, from us. You know better than that."

Frank didn't like seeing him like that. It was as if recent events had changed him from an easy, smart, and mellow man into something more like Nicky Spiro—a hood. Frank let him read the obligatory riot act. He took it all and said nothing, eyes averted.

Finally, Pojis slumped against the bar in Little Athens, shook his head. "Some things have been happening, Frank. You need to know about them. I took a few boys over to Johnny Six's place…"

Nicky owned the building Johnny Six lived in. He started getting complaints, Pojis said. Strange smells, sounds. All the tenants moved out of the fourth floor, refused to live there anymore. They said at night it was worse. Sounds of voices coming from Johnny Six's room, voices arguing and screaming and making sounds that weren't very pleasant to listen to. Nicky told Pojis to look into it, see what was going on.

"But I didn't tell Nick about what we knew," Pojis said. "I just couldn't bring myself to."

Frank decided that was probably a good thing.

"So we went up there," Pojis told him. "Me and two other guys. Real hardcases. Guys I knew I could trust. We were coming up the stairs and right away we smelled it.

This awful stink...like roadkill simmering on a hot plate. Odd, high, yeasty."

Pojis said it was ugly up there, walking down that corridor. The shadows were thick and crawling and they could hear a sloppy, slurping sound coming from behind Johnny Six's door. The three of them were carrying shotguns and they were ready for just about anything.

Pojis rapped on the door with the butt of his shotgun, told Johnny Six he better open that fucking door, he knew what was good for him.

And then they heard it, they all heard it: that voice. It was an eerie, wailing voice like an October wind trying to speak. "Get away...damn you...get away..."

The muscle Pojis had brought with him, local talent, looked ready to shit themselves. And these guys were hard as concrete, the sort that go after people with meat cleavers. Pojis himself was taking it no better. His mother's stories didn't begin to touch the reality of this. It was one thing to hear wild tales like that, but to actually witness them—

"I knew that voice, Frank," he explained, a rubbery yellow grin on his face. "I knew that voice real well. It was the freak, it was Gribbens...but windy and shrill like he was speaking from the bottom of a well."

The two hitters kicked the door in and that stench hit them full in the face like drainage from a slaughter yard.

"It was hot and black in there," Pojis told him, "just like you said. And, Christ, the windows were all boarded-up and right away I see this mess on the floor...this lumpy, slimy mess like somebody had slaughtered a moose, bloody and fleshy and stinking. Then that heap started moving, inching along the floor like a slug. That's when I knew it was Johnny Six. I could see his face spread out over its length, eyes open, Frank, open and aware of what had happened to him."

Pojis went on to say it was the most appalling thing he'd ever seen.

"I saw those eyes you were talking about, except it was worse, Frank, dear God it was much worse..."

And it was. There weren't just eyes now, but little brown replicas of the freak growing out of that creeping, cancerous mass that was Johnny Six. Dozens and dozens of them. Little twisted, dwarfed effigies with wasted pipe-cleaner arms and grinning, toothless mouths that spoke with high, squeaking versions of the freak's voice.

Pojis took a break. He was sweating and shaking like he had a good case of the flu going. He swallowed down brandy, using both hands to steady the glass. He licked his lips, his eyes red-rimmed and unblinking. "We...we started shooting 'em, Frank. We blew away twenty or more. And by the time we'd killed them, those other lumps and mounds and whatever the hell they were—like boils, they looked like boils—they started opening, splitting open like rotten eggs and more little freaks came out. But fetal and unformed, tearing through purple-veined placentas...and...and squealing like newborns...Christ, can you imagine it? Those boils opening like the buds of flowers and what came out, what blossomed..."

It took Frank a lot of brandy to get the rest out of him. "One of the hitters ran out and came back with a fire extinguisher. He sprayed Johnny Six down until he was white and stiff as an ice sculpture. And it was maddening looking at the boneless mass of him, all frosted-up and frozen tight, those little white-iced puppet versions of the freak trying to crawl out of him like worms from pork. They got more extinguishers and sprayed him down until he was frozen solid as January pavement. They bundled up the mass—one of the hardest things Pojis had ever done, he admitted—and dragged it downstairs. They took it to a foundry across the city and fed it into a blast furnace."

Pojis managed to light a cigar. "Where does this leave us?" he said, shaking his head. "Christ, if I know. This is a bad time for anything weird to be happening, Frank. Anything that might draw the wrong kind of attention to Greektown."

Frank knew what he was talking about. The big Greektown casino was up and operating nearby. Nicky Spiro was in on the whole thing along with the Italians. They had the skim going, they controlled the unions that controlled the workers. What Nicky didn't want was any prying eyes on him. Yeah, Frank knew about all that, but with what had been happening, he just couldn't give a shit about Nicky Spiro or his Mafia pals and their greed. All of that seemed so minor now, so unimportant.

Particularly with Johnny Six being dead. Christ. Pojis sighed. "There's a system to this, Frank. We both know that. Gribbens...he's out to get those who put him down. Those directly involved."

Frank nodded. "Johnny Six. Fat Pete. Maybe even Nicky because he gave the order. And me because, hey, I pulled the trigger."

"Me, too," Pojis said. "I interfered."

Frank sipped his drink, clutched Pojis by the shoulder. "I think," he said, "we better go see Fat Pete."

***

The sun was setting when they went in.

There were no lights on in Fat Pete's house. Maybe he hadn't paid the electric bill and maybe something else had decided it preferred the darkness. The damp, seething darkness where it could spawn and grow.

Frank and Pojis carried shotguns and 9mm Berettas as back-up. They brought two five-gallon jugs of kerosene with them. They stood in the entry and smelled the rich, ripe odor of decayed things, of organic profusion. Like the smell beneath a rotting log. The house was huge and shadowed and the silence was electric, loud. They went down the hallway towards the living room, a strange, almost savage energy in the air.

Frank kept telling himself that what he might see was not Fat Pete. Fat Pete was dead at best and at worst, a morbid nursery for the freak. And that's what it came down to. Gribbens refused to die, refused to accept that his life was over so he was re-birthing himself in the bodies of his assailants. Like some malefic, lunatic parasite he was draining them and re-generating himself. It was insane, but it was true.

That was his revenge.

They heard movement above, the creak of boards, the shift of timbers.

They mounted the stairway, racking the pumps of their shotguns, and started up side by side. The stairwell was black and grainy and it hid a multitude of sins. Their flashlight beams bobbed and swayed, creating eerie, prancing shadows. They were sweating and their hearts were pounding and it seemed hard to breathe.

Pojis said, "Don't mess around. You see it, just—"

But he never finished that for something immense and vicious came down the stairs at them in a flabby blur. And came so quick, they never got their flashlights on it. It slammed into them, pitching them down into the corridor. Frank's light was spinning in a tight circle, the house a crazy lantern show of dancing shadows and leaping shafts of light. Frank was looking and seeing…what? Shapes and forms and contorted faces. Maybe Pojis or Fat Pete or—

Pojis screamed and his shotgun went off once, blowing a hole in the wall.

Frank couldn't be sure what he saw, just something big on top of Pojis. He didn't dare shoot, so he threw himself at it, swinging his gun like a club. It was Fat Pete, he saw in a wink of illumination. Fat Pete was on top of Pojis, strangling him, choking the life out of him. Frank hammered at him, feeling bones pop and ribs cave-in and then he heard Pojis make an airless, grunting sound and his neck went with a wet snap and something struck Frank across the face and put him on his ass. The shotgun spun from his fingers.

But it was then, in the dim glow of Pojis' flashlight, that he really saw.

Fat Pete was dead. Or nearly. His body had been laying across Pojis', but he was beyond violence. He was like some fat, lolling spider that a wasp had tucked away in its burrow to flesh and feed its young. For rising directly out of Fat Pete's back, right between the shoulder blades, was Gribbens. Deformed, grotesque, leathery flesh the color of November leaves. His eyes were blazing yellow like searchlights cutting through fog, shriveled lips pulled back from blackened, angular teeth...and he was grinning with sadistic delight. He pulled those withered, skeletal fingers from Pojis' crushed throat and threw himself in Frank's direction. But it was no easy going; he wasn't fully formed. Beneath the hips, he was still fully joined to Fat

Pete. And when he moved, he had to drag that bulk with him.

Frank screamed and crab-crawled over the floor, his fingers closing over the stock of his shotgun just as the freak, hissing like a teakettle, took hold of his ankle and dragged him back as if he were stuffed with straw.

Frank rolled and brought the shotgun to bear. Gribbens screamed and then there was a deafening explosion as fire belched from the barrel. Buckshot slammed into the freak and vaporized his left arm and shoulder, splattering the stairway with blood and meat.

The freak shrieked and cawed and squealed and then Frank had him. He pounded on him with the butt of the shotgun, bringing it down again and again and again with a shattering impact that pulped Gribbens' bones and opened his skull and mashed his face into paste. Then he gave him every remaining round until there was nothing to mark the freak's passing but a gaping, smoking hole in Fat Pete's back.

Sometime later, Frank left.

A week after the police sifted through the ashes of Fat Pete's house and found some very disturbing bones that nearly turned the county coroner's hair white, Frank Vagris was living in a cheap room in Poletown. Poletown was a Polish/Eastern European enclave in Hamtramck. A working class neighborhood of immigrants, most of whom could speak little to no English.

And that was just fine with Frank.

Ever since he walked out of Fat Pete's blazing house, he'd been drinking. Whiskey, bourbon, beer, vodka, rum—it didn't much matter to him. He spent the week pickled as a lab specimen. And like that specimen, he floated in a soupy, alcoholic brine. No one in Poletown knew him. No one seemed to want to know him.

And that, again, was fine.

He lived in his little room, filthy, sweaty, chewing beef jerky and drinking. The only time he left was to get more booze. He had enough money to carry on like that for a few months, he figured.

Though, he knew, it wouldn't be that long.

Because certain choices were made for him.

Nicky Spiro had started it all in motion, putting the contract on Gribbens. And Frank knew he had to see him. Had to know—out of morbid curiosity, if nothing else—if the curse had gotten him, too.

So he went to see him.

***

Little Athens.

Nicky's restaurant. It was closed, sign said, until further notice. Nobody was around. Frank blew open the door in the alley, went in. He knew right away why the place was closed, why it had to be closed: the stink. A noisome stench of hot, moist growth. Nobody would eat there with that smell.

Nicky Spiro had rooms upstairs. Very lavish. When Frank got up there, the lights were out. Slime seeped from the deep-pile carpeting. The odor was stronger, pungent.

He found Nicky in bed, a wasted stick figure, so skinny he looked like something made out of coat hangers and paper mache. A lamp glowed at his bedside, turned down real low. Maybe because he didn't want people seeing what he'd become or didn't want to see himself.

"Frank," he said, his voice shallow and dry, barely even there. He pulled himself up, his skullish face like a dehydrated mask. "The freak…he did this to us, Frank. He did it…that fucking witch, that fucking devil…he did this."

"You think so?"

His head bobbed up and down. "I hear things."

Frank just nodded, his left hand itching horribly. "Revenge, Nicky. Because we whacked him—now it's just you and me."

But Nicky didn't give a shit about the others, about Frank. That was obvious. "Lookit me, Frank, lookit what he did to me."

Nicky was naked and Frank saw.

He thought about all the beautiful women Nicky had had. The models and starlets and society babes. All eager to make it with a tough hood like him, a guy who was powerful and dangerous.

But not a one of them would have touched him now.

For hanging between his legs was a little brown-skinned freak with yellow eyes and wiggling fingers. It grinned up at Frank, coiled with a sick, boneless motion like a fat graveworm.

If it hadn't been so damn horrible, it would have been funny. Nicky had always been proud of his dick. It was the center of who he was and what he was. And now—

"Kill me, Frank," Nicky whimpered. "Dear God, kill me."

Frank pulled the .38 out of his pocket, blew Nicky's skull to mucilage. The thing between his legs fought and squirmed, finally went still.

Frank's left hand began to itch madly.

He pulled it from his coat pocket where he kept it tucked away, unwrapping the bandages from it. There was no hand growing from his wrist, just a little fleshy replica of Gribbens. He stared at Frank with a mindless, cheated hatred. He knew what was going to happen...and he raged, filling Frank's brain with noise, trying to steal his thoughts, crush his free-will, take him over completely and make him his own. For he only needed a few more weeks, maybe a month and he would be re-born.

But it wasn't going to happen.

Frank started laughing, thinking what a good joke it was he was going to play on the freak. His hand itching, sending electric waves up into his shoulder, he put the muzzle of the .38 in his mouth and painted the ceiling with his brains. And the scream that was heard was not his, but that of something defeated, something that was simply out of options.

Gribbens, like his assailants, had run his course.

The End

Steerage Rats

By

Natasha Sinclair

The city of Glasgow was dying. History will glamorise an era of great depression because it was one soaked in recreational alcohol, hints of sexual liberation between men and women behind closed doors of those naughty, risqué Speakeasies - a somewhat rose-tinted view through a complicated history. The influence and perceived domination of the young Americas glossing over the rest of the world.

Point the lens across the ocean to this industrial city, where the picture was far bleaker. Local trade was being stamped out or swallowed up by beasts - monstrosities that were tearing at the workforce hard. Teeming with displaced men who didn't know what to do but work and go at it hard. When that was gone, a domino effect ensued as illegal vices and debauchery replaced the deeds of good honest men, until they had nothing.

Jim McKenzie was one such man, a man once surging with virility and pride who found his world falling fast. Further emasculation pained him when his wife, Jenny, suggested securing work while he helped with the kids. No, he couldn't have that, not as 'the man' of the house. In such turmoil at being as displaced from his home as he was in work, Jim found himself messing around with Jenny's sister, Betty.

Betty was younger, though she certainly wasn't ageing as well as her far more elegant, older sister, Jenny. Men gravitated towards Betty's playful, flirtatious nature, but none enough to stick around for very long. When hers left her unwed with a bairn in her belly five years back, she used those skills of flirtation to entice business, becoming somewhat of a passing place for many a man - making money the only way that made sense to her. Hanging around the shipyards picking up tricks who had more to lose, married Johns who knew to keep their vices quiet. She had always flirted with Jim, propositioning frequently enough that he knew the servicing would be free of coin – family privileges.

He had never been tempted until now. Knowing where Betty would be and when, desperate to feel some power again, a power he'd take from her. Of course, these things never quite work out that way. A little indiscretion or two with the good wife's sister threw another noose around his thick veiny neck, another threat sharpening its claws by the day, getting ready for the gullet. The slight swell of her belly hinting at another bastard, one that this time could be his, was becoming undeniable. Knowing she was not a stranger to such accidents and dealing with them discreetly, this was one she was not going to extinguish. She now held power over him, a guillotine with his exposed, taut neck tethered in wait beneath - her robed in black holding steady the rope. A fine tool to remove her sister's much coveted family head, with vindictive venomous delight. Such power sparked life in the little witch's heart. Still shaking her money-maker, knowing soon she could appeal to some fetishists who'd pay a little more for a go at her milky breasts, as he rutted on top of her.

Losing his job, financial stability, and routines, drinking more, gambling a bit, emasculation calcifying painfully in the pit of Jim McKenzie's acid clogged stomach and the in-family-indiscretion with its own accelerating threat - all of this cumulated in making Jim all the more desperate.

Back to the declining industrial, working man's landscape. The changes were a result of the borders of control closing in from the south thinning the population. There were even rumours of them sending up mutated monsters plagued with disease - just tall tales designed to scare, potentially. None the less, attacks from the devil's crown were unrelenting. With terrifying tales of rural villages being invaded and destroyed, spreading like wildfire, haunting the cities. Though many of the stories seemed too far-fetched to be true with talk not only of disease, but actual monsters tearing people limb from limb - tales for the gullible. Even still, across the country, city and country folk alike dreamed of independence from the south - this ran through the blood for centuries, embedding such maddening desire into the very DNA of all Scots. If they survived this century, that thirst would likely pour through the veins of the future for that independence; a profound craving to be free of the Lion.

Jenny McKenzie was a good woman - dedicated, strong and obedient in ways any married woman should be to her husband. With that, she couldn't refuse Jim; no 'good' woman does, and Jenny was every bit the by-the-book, perfect wife. When the man of the house gathered the family sternly announcing that it was time to leave, having secured work in Canada, along with safe passage - that was that. The family were emigrating, without discussion. From a man of steel in the shipyards to trapping and skinning, it seemed like a peculiar flip, but any honest paid work was not an offer to be refused. And Jim was indeed a desperate man. This offer was too good to miss – perhaps his only option aside from the real noose itself.

The sun was slow to rise on January 20th, 1926. Darkness enveloped a sluggishly exposed land. Gloomy dithering lethargy lingered, paining everyone on earth at the unrelenting despondency that deepened like winter. A weighty air supported heavy dirty hands over the mouth and nose – breathing now impossible.

Lives carefully packed in a few small suitcases at the docks, the kids were excited for adventure, welcomingly taking the edge off Jenny's quiet tentativeness about such a tremendous upheaval. Jim, of course, couldn't be more eager to escape.

The Anchor & Donaldson Liner was breath-taking as she sat magnificent and proud by the bustling industrial Clydeside. The children were mesmerised, at least Jimmy and Maggie were, baby Billy didn't seem to notice the fuss - tucked firmly by his mother's breast, nothing phased the infant. It was both intriguing and terrifying to journey upon such an astounding piece of engineering - vessels entirely constructed by the rough hardworking hands of men like their father. Now, their voyage on one of these colossal vessels, the SS Kentigern, would take them beyond the skyline to a new life far from the only lands they knew across the mysterious, vast ocean.

Canada was the land of hope. Families reunited went on to build; reimagining themselves no longer slaves to the south but as men who made their own fortune; commanders of land, respected, men who could look their wives in the eye, men who felt free to live and love again.

Crammed in 3rd class, miserable but clean - it had everything that they needed, and lady luck did provide a four-berth stateroom in steerage; a relative and rare luxury. This ship was merely a passing place between lives, old to new. Suspending its passengers in limbo; a ship of mourning and hope.

The McKenzie family got to know many passengers travelling to the new world in 3rd class that first week on board. The 1st could be seen looking down on dry, bright days from the wrap-around decks above with either alien-like curiosity or god-like arrogance. Of course, there was no mixing - repulsion and envy make unlikely bedfellows when the idea of the elite fraternising with the riff-raff rats of steerage was aroused.

At home amongst 'their own' the McKenzies shared camaraderie with the experiences walking the lower corridors, even from those who boarded at Liverpool and Belfast, making friends quickly. Jim would play cards after dinner most nights while Jenny got the kids to sleep and tended to little Jimmy, who had trouble adjusting to sea life. Something especially challenging in the bowels of the ship where the air had quickly staled. The eight-year-old was struck with seasickness, at least that was the assumed culprit.

After a rough day at sea, Jenny returned with the children to their stateroom to settle them in bed early. Jimmy was sickly green, and all were exhausted from the constant movement. There was no place to be still here though there was nowhere to go. With the body in continuous nauseating motion when still, it was a wonder more didn't suffer the sickness. Jenny tucked little Maggie first in the bottom bunk, then Jimmy on the upper bunk adjacent before getting into her own above Maggie. Nursing baby Billy to sleep as she quietly sang, her warm, soft Celtic sonnet soothed the children with ease. Their mother's voice was home no matter the place, lulling them all to sleep as the boat rolled and creaked, slicing steel blades through the deep dark Atlantic.

What was that noise? Jenny's body trembled as an otherworldly sound woke her from a dead-exhausted-sleep. Wet, sloppy lapping then crazed crunching like some ravenous animal chewing down on chicken bones – snapping and cracking. Sitting up and peering over to the next bunk, Jenny's eyes caught the light bounce of something dark and wet with some strange dark shape moving above. Then her brain started to make sense of the horror before her; a monstrous, overgrown rat, the size of a large bull terrier dog was perched on top of Jimmy's chest. The beast's long tail hung off the side, thick and scaly, excitedly tapping the metal floor with the tip. Chewing its way through the child's cheek. Half of Jimmy's face was sunken in; there was no skin, only darkness. What little light there was, seeping in from the edges of the slightly ajar door, bounced harshly off exposed broken, bloody, jawbones and baby teeth. As Jenny's mind struggled to make sense of this gruesome sight, the giant ears twitched, the rat-beast turned its horrifying blood-soaked face towards her - snout, whiskers and fangs dripping with the insides of little Jimmy's half-eaten face. Jenny screamed, inaudibly as no sound left her mouth - her delicate throat paralysed in shock and fear.

Her mind ran in frantic bursts. Time transforms so very different in the mind; *Jimmy isn't moving. His face is gone! My god, my baby's face! He can't possibly be alive. I could try to get Jimmy out but without any weapon to fend off the beast I'd be risking the death of the other two children. Or save them first? Jimmy is already dead, and that seems to be the rat-beasts' distraction from the others in the room. What the hell is that thing! Just move! Get help and come back for Jimmy.* Logic seemed to take over above feeling for her obviously, dead son. As with oil and water, emotion rarely marries logic, a failure of a blend, molecules crashing but never connecting.

Tormented, she scrambled scooping up Billy who was still sound asleep by her and dropped off the side of the bunk. Bare feet hitting the cold floor, she slipped on some blood, landing hard on her back with the baby on her chest. Jimmy's blood! My babies blood! Pain and terror pounded its way up her pelvis through her spine as she screamed inside her head - screaming echoes rattled within her skull as it would in a tin box. The rat-beast nonchalantly turned and continued to eat through Jimmy's face. With chilling calm, it had no fear of her. Reaching, Jenny tapped furiously at the blankets to wake Maggie, shushing her, she pulled the four-year-old girl from the bed and made for the door. Escaping the cabin and shutting the stiff, rusting, white-painted steel door, Jenny with a child in each arm got to her feet and pelted barefoot down the narrow, flickering-low-lit, bare corridor toward the stairwell. Turning left, she ran until she reached the communal room at the end.

***

"Well, Geo boy, it's about that time." Harry tipped his head towards the clock upon the grand mahogany mantel of the elegant 1st class smoking room, before taking a long drag of his thick hand-rolled Cuban. Rolling the flavours around his mouth with his fat tongue before immersing his face in the smoke that now billowed from his lips, a sly grin tickling the edges. Rhythmic ticks had been enchanting the room with promise for some time now. *Tick. Tick. Tick. Tick.* Midnight drawing closer.

George sucked the air in through his teeth, eager. "Yes sir." Perching uncomfortably on the edge of one of the high-backed well-worn red velvet chairs arranged around a round oak table by the large mantel. He was well aware his time was near. This was his second crossing with The Agency, he understood the procedure to be completed before reaching Toronto. Although he wore a skin-tight layer beneath the protective suit, the outer suit still made his skin itch, that or the nerves were creating a distraction from his imminent task. *Hurry up Ron, Hurry the fuck up!* Externally he was trying to remain professional, controlled, unfaltering. His partner for the job, Ron, had been gone for almost 40 minutes, double what George expected - those extra minutes stewed in his mind, agitating. Trying not to panic about all the things that could go wrong - the more time that passed, the more he wanted to scratch. A young man he may well be, but he wasn't naïve, knowing he was as disposable as anyone else. Get the job done, so you don't become 'the job.'

"Don't worry boy, he'll be back in a jiffy. Have a drink." Harry handed George a heavy-bottomed crystal glass of liquor. "It's good stuff this. You'll not get it just anywhere boy, go on knock this back, it'll sort you out."

"Thank you, sir" George threw the glass of amber liquid down his throat, it sent a fire like adrenaline through him instantly, sharpening his wavering internal motors.

The failed experimental critters had been left hungry enough without access to food for a little more than a week. Crazed now, they were edging close to cannibalising one another, that's when a hatch was opened earlier that evening, steering them up from a secret cargo hold towards the 3rd class berths. By now, those low worth passengers that had bedded down should be dead or close to, and those that hadn't would no doubt swarm together to try overcoming their bloody fate. Cattle to the slaughter. They wouldn't make it, they never did - and a tragedy at sea wasn't unusual. Nor were vanishing passenger lists. The truth of what goes on at sea stays at sea, as with the goings-on amongst men.

"Well, you should get the rest of the gear on boy, I can hear them boots in the passage."

At that, the brass handle of the door clicked, and Ron walked in, awkward from the all in one black protective suit rustling around him, like some sort of astronaut. Pulling the mask and hood from his face over his head, panting, "Right, they're in, all exits are locked down bar one, and I checked in with Bobbie and John there, they've checked and shut in the private rooms - just the one general room left for me and the young Geo."

"You hear that boy, time to get your hands dirty so to speak. Ok, Ron you know what to do. Clean ship boys!" He winked and stuck the Cuban back between his chubby lips.

Clearing his throat, George grabbed his mask and followed Ron back out down the passage as they headed for steerage.

"It'll be an easy one mate. We can just light 'em up and lock 'em in. Then muck in with the clean-up crew in a few hours. I've got the immobilising device for the critters if we need it."

They took the elevator down to 2nd class, exiting next to crew apartments there at the stern of the ship. Ron had already prepared the equipment that they needed.

"Sounds solid. Masks on now?"

"Yes, and tuck that goddam leg into your boot while you're at it – you don't want any of those rats finding a way inside, especially if one hasn't eaten yet."

"Thanks mate." All geared up, George grabbed the hose reel which was already attached to the fuel, and they made for the stairwell that would take them to the lower deck - snaking the hose reel down behind.

"Ready?" Ron's voice was firm and assuring to his new teammate.

"Ready."

***

Pushing the handle with her elbow, Jenny shoved through the door with her full weight using her shoulder and hips. She stumbled into the room collapsing with the children, a heap on the floor. She let out a wail then, a high-pitched squeal that was almost inhuman, the sound of a mother's heart-shattering. The screech was like a million shards of glass being thrust into the ears, echoing around the room. Deafening.

"It ate Jimmy's face! My baby! Oh, my baby! It ate him!" She screamed choking on her hysteria as the bustling smoky room fell silent to her cries.

"Jenny?!" Jim broke through the crowd making haste for his distraught family, wrapping his arms around her as two other women came and coddled the children from Jenny's arms. "You're not making any sense woman, where's little Jimmy? He asleep?"

"Didn't you hear me! It ate his face Jim! That thing. That monster! It was eating our Jimmy's face!" She pointed, shaking towards where she had come in, as she did, scurrying could be heard from the corridor - catching everyone's attention as it picked up speed. All eyes turned from the hysterical woman on the floor to the door behind her. The Scurrying and tapping got louder then, and dark shadows where being cast at the end of the passageway, then they saw them - turning the corridor heading straight for them - so many rats! A rumbling wave of ghastly fur rolled towards them, skittering growing ever more rapid. Amongst them, there were rodents the size of dogs, mutated, angry, rabid slobbering and petrifying! Those galloped more than skittered.

"What the hell?!" Some murmured as a few of the men ran to shut the door.

"Why are there so many of them?" Came another voice.

"Forget that, we're used to some rats down here but what the hell was wrong with the bigger beasts?! I've never heard of a rat that size!" Called Pete, one of the Liverpudlians Jim had been playing cards with.

Thuds thrummed against the steel door. It sounded like they were throwing themselves at it, or that the beasts hadn't slowed down quick enough to stop before bodies hit metal. Pelting against the steel like a furious hale. Thuds were fast followed by frenzied scratching. Trapped, there was no other way out.

In the panic, someone came up with the only solution that seemed like it could work – Fire. With a plentiful supply of strong alcohol and plenty of matches, if they could just burn through enough of the rats to escape the room and make for the upper decks - it was either that or wait, and for what they did not know. A couple of the more organised started gathering up and handing out bottles of liquor, passing it around the room of an easy fifty folk, those who didn't have alcohol to douse the beasts with loaded up with matches. All lined up in rough rows facing the door as Pete, who seemed the only one brave or daft enough to volunteer to open the door, braced himself behind the steel as the crazed scratching and squeaking continued vibrating insanity through the metal.

"Right. This is it, folks. Let's do this!" He breathed in deeply puffing out his broad chest. "After three. One. Two. THREE!" He wrenched the door open. A swarm of fur poured in - a ghastly rat-tsunami of terror. Glass bottles of whisky, ale, and rum were thrown toward the terrifying tumbling mass. Screaming ensued from the sheer horror of it all. There were some whose bodies were swarmed with rats before they could contribute to the fight. The crazed blood-mad swarm was eating them alive. Tearing out chunks of flesh and burrowing deep inside, infesting their victims with their dirty wet furry little bodies to continue feasting from the inside. Those inside their fallen victims could be seen rolling around in a frenzy beneath the skin; a truly revolting sight of human skin stretched over frenzied rats like a taut blanket as they fought just beneath burying deeper still into the flesh and organs. Blood and chunks of flesh spattered the wood-planked floors and walls. Amongst it all, lit matches were being thrown towards the door, setting some of the beasts alight. It didn't slow them down; it seemed to make them more frenzied as balls of blood-crazed, booze-soaked, burning fire-ball rats threw themselves onto more men and women all the faster. Some of those who tried to make their great escape towards the only exit slipped on the bloody, alcohol-soaked floors and immediately were overrun and consumed by the psychotic critters.

Jenny huddled at the back with the two women who had taken Maggie and Billy when she entered the room. The three women shielded the children with their bodies - backs against them trapped in the corner. Jenny had lost track of where Jim was in the fray, frantically searching the chaos she caught sight of a burning man screaming and flailing, running towards the door, recognising Jim's checked trousers - the screaming, burning man was her husband. As he reached the door, two huge shapes appear outside it, and one pokes combusting Jim back into the room with a huge metal stick, causing him to tumble to the floor.

They appeared to be men, wearing black full-body protective suits with huge gas-style-masks over their faces, only their beady-cold-calm eyes visible. They both turn and nod to one another, the man on the right produces a hose and begins to spray fluid into the room, speeding up the ignition. The other then reaches in, unphased, firmly pulling shut the heavy door.

Flames and heat tumble and roll, roaring towards Jenny straight into her face. She feels her skin frazzle, melt, and burn. Dry searing pain consuming, melting her eyeballs which pop and explode inside her flaming head. Flame, blood and terror engulfs all life - a tidal wave pulling limbo fast from dreams of elevated hope to terrors of an ever-burning hell.

The End

Blood for Blood

By

Zoey Xolton

Chest heaving, I catch my breath in erratic gasps. My mind is spinning, and for just a moment, I fail to make sense of the scene before me. The bloody knife in my hand clatters to the uneven floorboards as my body trembles with unbridled rage. My off-white shift is stained red, like my soul—the walls, and even the roof above, too. On the floor before me, laying butchered in a foul mess of his own excrement, is my step-brother.

For what seems a lifetime I just stand there, eyes-wide as I drink in the vengeance I have meted out. I admire the irregular, frantic array of gashes that pepper his once pretty flesh; a stab, hilt-deep, for every time that he defiled me, and took me against my will. I had been innocent once, but it seems hard to recall. He'd begun his sick and depraved attacks against me from the moment I had become of marriageable age.

I can almost hear his hot breath against my ear, still.

"Why should father sell you off like some cow, when I can have you all to myself?"

The physical memory of his hand at my throat, as his other reached beneath my coverings with practised skill, too near. I double-over, my body reacting of its own volition at the thought, and I add the contents of my stomach to the macabre display. On my hands and knees, I wipe my mouth with the back of my sleeve, and give myself a minute, allowing myself to regain my composure.

"You'll never hurt me again," I hiss through my teeth, finally. I gaze upon his cruel, handsome face, and I feel a maniacal grin split my own. "Your turn to choke on it, Henry" I say, taking pleasure in the way his severed cock hangs limply from his mouth. An uncontrollable sense of relief washes over me, and I begin to laugh. It begins as a nervous giggle, before transforming into a fit of hysterical laughter, and that's how they find me; my family, and our neighbours. Splattered, covered head to toe in blood, a cackling, broken wretch at my dead step-brother's side.

I hear my mother gasp as she faints. My step-father looks down upon me, and in my post-murder delirium I see the rage of Hell itself behind his eyes. His face turns beetroot red, and he looks as if he will explode. I have taken his eldest son from him. He wants to kill me, I can see it as plainly as day. Our horrified neighbours make the sign of the cross, and usher the children who'd followed, from our humble home. All the while Richard just stands there, the darkness, and palpable hatred in him filling the desecrated room.

"Throw her in the larder," he barks, and two of our young male farm-hands seize me by the arms, and begin dragging me to my temporary prison. I do not resist. I have not the strength for it, and it doesn't matter now. Whatever becomes of me, my will has been done—justice has been served—and they can't take that away from me. Henry can't hurt me anymore, nor will he ever lay a hand upon my sisters. I have no regrets.

As I am moved past my step-father he glares at me with the fury of God, himself.

"You will rue the day you took my son from me, girl," he spits, and with a wave of his hand I am cast off, tossed into the larder, and the door latched firmly behind me.

"Gather the council, and summon the village. Tonight this little slut will burn!" I hear Richard order. A small voice inside me whispers that I should panic, that I should spend what little time I have left on this Earth malingering in fear...but I will not. Instead, I succumb gratefully to exhaustion, and forsake my concerns. For the first time in years, I am at peace when I sleep.

***

When I come to, I am being dragged through the village. My feet are bare, and my hands are bound. I am still in my torn undergarments rank with blood—the evidence of my crime. The sky is now black, and the stars are out, the village square lit only by torch light.

"Burn the witch!" I hear. "Murderer!" and "send her to Hell!" follow.

Soon the gathered populace of Salem is jeering, even the women and children are spitting as we pass...people I know, and have grown up with, supposedly *good* people. I wince when I see the pyre ahead being prepared, extra bundles of kindling added, and being doused with oil.

It hits me. This is my funeral procession, and I am going to my death. There will be no trial, or chance to speak my truth, to reveal what a lecherous, incestuous monster Henry was. They have made up their minds, all of them, these followers of Christ. They who attend Sunday Mass, and claim to uphold all His laws. As the pyre looms nearer I search the sea of familiar faces. I see blasphemers, thieves, gamblers, husbands who have mistresses, and church leaders who have paid for their victims' silence. None of them are innocent, or without sin, yet it is I who will burn.

Sucking in a lungful of the crisp night air, I find my feet and dignity. I hold my head high as I am man-handled up the stairs of the make-shift platform. With fierce courage I stand before the stake, holding back my tears as my hands are jerked above my head, and secured. They bind me at the waist, and feet with rope, and my fate is tied to that of the wooden beam at my back, as surely as the fate of the moon is tied to the sun.

My long, dirty blonde hair, mussed and caked with blood, hangs in my eyes as the first voice rises above the din, commanding silence.

"Tonight we gather to seek justice for Henry Blackwell, his life cut tragically short by this woman."

The crowd jeers, eager for retribution. Seemingly satisfied with the villagers' umbrage, the bishop raises his hand, and the crowd quiets once more. "Amity Williams, you have been found guilty of murder, and heresy; your own family, and God-fearing neighbours having born witness to your heinous crime. Let it be known that you butchered your step-brother, and severed his member for use in blood magic! You have been found a witch, guilty of witchcraft, and your sins must be atoned in blood. You are sentenced to death by burning. The fire will cleanse your wanton soul, and perhaps God, in his infinite wisdom and mercy, will grant your soul clemency when you have paid for the life you have stolen this day!"

The roar from the crowd is deafening as they raise their torches in the gloom.

My eyes roam the sea of heckling faces, and I find not one that is sympathetic. Even the faces of the little ones are contorted in ghoulish mockeries of their parents' umbrage. They know not what they are even shouting for. My step-father stands by the bishop, his face set like stone—he holds an unlit torch. My mother is nowhere to be seen. I let my head rest against the stake for a moment, and let their hate wash over me.

When I next open my eyes, a glint in the darkness beyond the baying crowd catches my attention. I peer into the night, past the flickering torchlight, and for several lung-aching moments I forget how to breathe. An impossibly beautiful man watches intently from the shadows, his black wings reflecting the pale moonlight, as his silver-blue eyes bore into my soul.

He is an angel! I realise in awe.

"And a Fallen one, at that," I hear in my mind.

I gasp internally. *"You're not here to take me to Heaven,* then..." I respond.

"I'm afraid not, child. Your God has forsaken you, but rest assured, you will come to no harm by my hand. I am Lucifer, and I am here to claim you."

"It isn't fair," I answer, defiantly holding back my tears. *"They are all as guilty as I, if not more!"*

Lucifer smiles. *"Indeed they are. You have my word, dear girl, they will suffer for their sins for all eternity, and you will be there to bear witness."*

I exhale, and smile at the thought. *"I would like that very much."*

"The witch dares to smile!" someone shouts, breaking me from our mind-to-mind conversation. The the rabble rises again. A few men stalk toward the pyre, and I am sobered by the splash of the oil as it drenches my feet, soaking the hem of my shift.

"Where is my mother?" I call out, hoping to perhaps say goodbye.

Richard steps forward, a sadistic leer stretching across his face. "Her soft heart could not bear the shame of your wickedness child. I am here in her stead to see that you leave this life, screaming."

Our eyes lock and we stare at one another in abject hatred. My step-father reaches out then, touching his torch to another's, and approaches. "For Henry," he says aloud, before tossing it onto the pyre. I steady my breathing as the fire races to form a circle around me, following and devouring the trail of pitch.

As the flames dance higher, taking hold of the kindling, I see Lucifer awaiting me in the darkness.

"Do not be afraid. It will hurt, more than anything you have ever known, but it will be short-lived."

The heat haze begins to rise as the fire grows in intensity. The villagers watch on intently with sick delight.

Richard's eyes have not left my face. He wants to witness my suffering, right down to the last exquisite moment of agony.

Bastard. "Step-father," I call above the flames. "It is just as well that your Henry did not live to marry. He had a rather small cock, I'm afraid! I doubt he would have served his wife-to-be, well." I grin until my face hurts, and I can all but tangibly see steam fuming from Richard's ears. There are whispers among the crowd, and the bishop gestures to his men. They rush forward with re-filled buckets and douse me with oil, momentarily blinding me.

Just as Lucifer had promised, my end comes relatively fast. The flames climb quickly, writhing up my body to embrace me like the lover I never knew. The fire burns, engulfing me. It scorches my flesh black, as the fat beneath bubbles and drips where my skin splits; my hair, and lashes are gone in an instant. I scream, and scream, until my voice breaks, and the very air is stolen from my charred, bleeding lungs.

There is no one, and nothing, but the agony. I have never known such pain. Every fibre of my being hurts. I feel my lips melt, and my eyelids sear away—the fluid in my eyes boiling inside my skull. A single heartbeat later and my head falls forward. Amity of the flesh is gone, and my corpse—no more than a human torch—burns brightly in the night.

***

I am standing in the shadows, watching my earthly encasement immolate. The cool night air is rank with the pungent odour of burnt meat. Sparks fly up into the darkness, buoyed by the pillar of hot smoke, and the villagers who had been jeering just moments before have fallen silent now. They stand in a crowd around the pyre like sentinels. It seems no one is bold enough to be the first to leave.

"Are you ready, Amity?" says Lucifer aloud. He extends his hand, and with one last glance back at the fire, at what was once me, I take it. His fingers wrap around mine and he smiles.

I nod. "I believe so. There is nothing here for me now. Maybe I was always destined for damnation."

"It's not as bad as they say," he promises as a yawning black portal opens before us.

"Hell, the Kingdom of the Damned and Forsaken, not as bad?"

"The very same," he says. "It is only as bad as those who enter it deserve. And you, sweet child, have suffered enough. Your Blood has been repaid, and now, I have a task in mind for you, should you choose to accept it."

"What sort of task?" I ask, as we step into the darkness.

Lucifer squeezes my hand, his eyes soft and reassuring. "Let me show you. I think you'll enjoy it."

***

"Welcome to my kingdom," says Lucifer.

I can only stare in awe at the vast, glittering vision before me. In the distance a great black castle towers over the landscape, and there are as many grand houses as there are stars in the sky. Paved streets, so unlike the peasant dirt roads of my village, are lined with strange, but exotically beautiful gardens. In the distance, there are winding rivers that sparkle, as if liquid silver were poured onto the landscape with an artist's eye.

Beyond it all, the skyline glows, as if the sun lays dying just out of sight; the ether above a magnificent array of hues—magenta, violet and indigo, fading into a midnight blue that bleeds into an inky, all-encompassing black.

Lucifer watches me intently. I can see that he takes pleasure in my astonishment.

"It is more enchanting than anything I could have ever dreamed," I say finally, when I can find the words.

"It pleases me that you appreciate my art."

"Is this truly Hell? I cannot believe it. The bishops preached to us of the infernal fires, and the nightmares of The Pit. This is...like a kingdom of perpetual night; dark, but alluring. It's peaceful."

The King of Hell nods almost imperceptively. "You are well spoken. You can read."

"My mother taught me," I acknowledge proudly. "Books were forbidden by the Church, but mother shared stories of magic, love, and adventure with me in secret. If you were found with a book, you were made a spectacle of in the village square. The book would be burned, and the one guilty of coveting such sacrilege would receive five lashes." I fall silent as I am overcome with the memory.

Lucifer waits.

"My mother was lashed in my stead, when I was discovered in the woods by a neighbour as I read. She took the blame...said it was hers, and that my straying from the laws of the Church was her failing alone."

"I know," says the Fallen angel. "Salem reeks with corruption and sin, most of it enacted in the name of God. Many have suffered, as you did, as your mother has."

I grimace, sullen and contemplative.

"Come now, this is your new home. You are welcome to dwell here, or within the walls of my castle, if you prefer; but I feel it is time to reveal to you the dark underbelly of Hell...and it is so much more than your priests and bishops knew."

"There's more?"

"Indeed. This is my Eden, Amity, the upper level of Hell, where the wrongly damned live according to their own will and desires. Within my keep dwells the Shadow Court; but far below, in the bowels of my kingdom, there are many levels of torment and atonement."

"Am I to be tortured? Must I repent?"

"Far from it, child. As I said, your debt is paid. Your only crimes were the pursuit of knowledge, and having a spirit of curiosity, and rebellion. And there is anger in you, a fire that sparks and feeds on injustice! I would see this gift put to good use."

I feel an uncertain, but curious smile alight upon my face, and I bite my lip. "I would be honoured to serve you, my Lord."

Lucifer takes my hand, again. "Come then, it is to the first level of The Pit we go—to the eternal realm of those who have committed the Sin of Lust."

***

In a swirl of midnight mist we appear in what appears to be an immense, underground cavern—a prison. The floor, walls and endless levels above, are hewn from a smooth, reflective black rock. We are at the bottom, at the centre of this place. Before us, a throne hewn from the very floor sits upon a dais, torches burning on either side. Two silent, grotesque, towering creatures in armour stand guard.

"What are they?" I ask.

"They are the Guardians of the First Prince, or Princess."

My brown furrows. "And who sits there?"

Lucifer side-eyes me. "That is where you come in, Amity."

I feel my eyes bulge, and I can't believe what I'm hearing. "I don't understand," I begin.

Lucifer cuts me off with an impish grin. "Yes, you do. It is there in your mind, already. This is *your* throne, should you wish to accept my offer."

I swallow hard. "My throne..."

"You were a victim in life of the debaucheries of Lust. You know its touch, its feel. You intimately understand its taint. You know what it is to be someone's plaything."

The memories of my abuse flood back and I feel the rage in my heart rekindled.

"Every level of Hell needs a ruler to enact the penalties of the wicked, and to ensure that justice is met.

There are many positions of duty, but at its heart, the one who sits upon the throne is the one who has the final word. All others are subservient to the First Princess on this level. The Guardians, the Punishers, and all the demons under my thrall will obey you, here. The Princes and Princesses of the other levels cannot contest you here."

"I am to be a princess?" My mind reels. "A princess of Hell..."

"I understand it is a lot to absorb. There is royalty here, the House of Morningstar, my house, and nobility. We have armies, and therefore ranked warriors, and generals of war. You will not be *The* Princess of Hell, but you will be The Princess of Lust, one of the Seven Stewards of Sin. You will hold a position at Court, and be heard on matters pertaining to the running of the kingdom."

I must look as taken aback and flabbergasted as I feel, because Lucifer stops, and takes me by the shoulders. "You are under no obligation to accept this offer. If you so wish, you can simply spend eternity in

Eden. You can sing, dance, read, find love...however, if you would like to see true sinners punished for the harm they have caused innocent souls, then you will find the position both empowering and, dare I say it, darkly enjoyable."

I already know what I want, before I have the strength to voice it. A chance to ensure that the suffering of the innocent—souls, just like me—does not go unpunished, is too great an opportunity to refuse.

"I do not know what strength I have in me, my Lord, but I would be your hand of retribution, if you think me up to the task."

Lucifer steps back, his long black hair gleaming in the flickering torch light. "You were born to punish the wicked, Amity. This is your rebirth. Behold."

Black flame spontaneously envelops me, and I feel the fear within burning away. My doubts, my weaknesses, they evaporate in blazing heat of the glorious inferno. My skin tingles all over, and my sad, stained shift falls away in cinders. I gasp, as I feel all traces of the victim from Salem stripped away, leaving nothing but strength, conviction, power and an insatiable hunger for justice.

When the flames die away, I behold my reflection in the polished stone of the throne. I approach it, my hands straying to my face, before trailing down my chest and sides. I am flawless, the most breath-taking me I could possibly be. My hair falls in a river of liquid gold, and my once pale flesh is bronzed. My once thin, undernourished frame is lean, toned and strong; and my eyes, they are as black as moonless night.

I turn to the King of Hell, unashamed. I don't think I could feel such an emotion as anything more than a memory, even if I tried. "I am beautiful," I utter.

"You always were," says Lucifer, "only now, you are a princess." With a snap of his fingers I feel myself clothed, adorned in a costume that fits from toe to neck like a second skin. The material, finer and more pliant than any leather I had seen in life indulges my every curve. My hair twists into what feels to be a braid, and perfectly comfortable boots enclose my feet.

Lucifer approaches, beholding his work of art. "Come," he says, and taking my hand, he leads me to the throne. Taking a deep breath I sit down.

"Now that you are reborn, a true reflection of your innermost soul, would you like to select a new name, one of your own choosing, to live henceforth, in Hell?"

I feel myself void of an idea of where to begin with deciding upon something as sacred as a new name. "I cannot choose, my Lord. I lived but a short time, and my knowledge of the wider world is limited. It would be an honour if you would bequeath me with one."

The darkly radiant Fallen angel ponders but a moment, before dragging a sharp, black nail across his own palm. Stepping forward, he anoints my brow with his angelic blood. By his strokes I feel that he has drawn the inverted cross. "Rise now, Naamahna, I name you in honour of one of the Four Queens of Hell, a succubus of the Void, and one of the women who led Adam to stray from God, himself."

I stand, and feel awash with power. It flows through me, throbbing within my immortal veins. I feel hate fill my soul. *Lucifer is truly my Lord. God made a victim of me, but Lucifer made me a princess.*

"Sinners!" Lucifer purrs, his voice amplified for all the level to hear. "Behold your new mistress, the First Princess of Lust! Your damnation, and salvation lie within her hands!"

A flaming whip of plaited gold materialises in the palm of my right hand. I touch its burning length, but feel no pain. I return Lucifer's sly grin, and with a thought, the whip coils at my waist.

"Naamahna," he says, curling a finger. "I have one final gift for you, before your coronation at Court. Consider it a 'welcome home', gift."

I feel my eyebrows reach for my hairline in query, but follow on in quiet curiosity.

"You can now travel within the eight realms of Hell at will, with no more than a thought," he informs me over his shoulder. "You need only think on where you want to be, or with whom you want to be with, and you will appear at your desired destination. Try it, focus on me."

The heart-achingly beautiful King vanishes from sight, leaving me alone with the guards in the throne room.

Taking a deep breath, I visualise Lucifer, and focus my intent. An instant later and I am by his side, standing outside of a barred prison cell. The walls of the immaculate cell glitter with a breath-taking array of metallic implements. Glinting, cruel knives in all shapes and sizes, cleavers, axes, large collections of pins, hammers, and other interesting things I don't have names for, abound.

"The tools of your accursed trade, Princess Naamahna," says Lucifer, following my eye.

At the centre of it all, a large, solid block of stone. Upon it, a young man is shackled by his wrists and ankles. I open my mouth to speak, to ask whom this is, when I realise that I already know. I hold my breath, scarcely daring to hope. I approach the bars, and to me, they shimmer, almost imperceptibly. Trusting my instincts, I step forward, passing through the bars as if they were not there at all.

I approach the stone and gaze down upon the face of my once nightmare—the twisted soul of the one whom claimed my precious innocence. "Henry." The names slips from my lips, the bastard stirs, his body tensing.

"It's not a voice you can forget, is it?" I ask, my eyes boring into his soul.

He stares back, eyes wide, full of confusion and terror.

"Amity," he whispers in disbelief.

Lucifer appears by my side, and Henry shrinks away against the stone. "You will address her as Mistress Naamahna, sinner. Her name will be the only prayer on your lips from now, until the end of eternity. Is that clear?"

The infernal fires of Hell blaze in the King's eyes and Henry pisses himself.

"Yes, Great Satan," he utters in abject horror.

Lucifer smiles, leaning against the stone casually. "It will take a handful of hours to prepare the castle and Court for your coronation," he says.

My eyes never leave Henry's face.

Lucifer's grin is delightfully wicked. "I'll leave you two to become reacquainted." Placing a hand on my shoulder, he gives it a gentle squeeze. "Enjoy, Princess, I'll return in due course."

I meet his eye and feel every bit the demon I have become. "Take your time," I insist. "Henry and I have much to discuss."

Lucifer vanishes in a trail of swirling black mist, and we are finally alone.

I walk the length of the room, making a show of trailing my fingers along the beautiful tools of my trade, before finally selecting a sinister, thin, curved blade. I bite my lip, vicious glee surging within me. "It seems the tables have turned," I drawl, as I stride slowly toward him. He looks so beautiful laying there, so prone and helpless. "It's time you understood how it feels to be a victim."

Henry's eyes fill with tears of self-pity as he whimpers.

I smile, shushing him.

"There, there," I whisper, bending down, and leaning in close. I lick the length of his face, before teasing his ear between my teeth. I can taste his fear. "Don't cry, love. You wanted to play with me, you said so yourself; and now, we shall play—*forever*."

The End

Book Magic

By

Kevin J. Kennedy

I'm not quite sure why, but books spoke to me from a young age. I think I was seven or eight years old and they started a book club in my school. You would give your teacher money when you had it and they noted it in a little book, almost like an old bank book. Once a week they would give out a colour, four-page pamphlet showing you all the books you would be able to buy when the book club came around. From memory, they came to the school twice a year.

I used to take half of my lunch money each day and give it to my teacher. None of the other kids seemed interested. If they kept some of their lunch money, it was to buy stickers for the latest sticker album or Garbage Pail Kids cards or sometimes to add to their pocket money, to buy a better toy. I liked all of those things, but the colourful pictures of all the books that would be available just called out to me.

Neither my mother or father were readers. Well, apart from the newspaper that is. I don't think I knew anyone who read books, but I knew I needed to get some.

Our school had taken us on a trip to the library once at that point and I found it to be a magical place. I couldn't borrow any books though as I didn't have a library card. We lived quite far away from it and my parents didn't drive so they never did join. I knew I would have to buy my books and for that, I would need to save.

When the people who sent us the book pamphlet finally arrived for the first time, I was amazed. They had been given the gym hall to set up. They had brought with them several bookshelves that were on wheels and had lined them up in rows with all the bright shiny new books displayed on them. Even though the gym hall usually smelled of sweat, I could smell a different smell as I walked between the rows. It was like the smell of the library but newer. It felt like home.

I bought ten times as many books that first time they came, as any other kid in the school. I had to sneak the books into my room in my school bag, so my parents

didn't realise that I wasn't spending my lunch money on food. For the next few weeks I immersed myself in Goosebumps, Point Horror and The Worst Witch books. Oh, and I got a few Roald Dahl ones too. They were all magical. They transported me to another world.

It didn't take me long to get through the books, but I knew I needed more. No way could I spend my evenings having such pleasure and go back to watching stupid shows on the television. We had a school library, but it was small, and all of the books were ancient. I went along anyway and told the librarian what I had been reading and enjoying and she suggested a few books for me. I borrowed The Time Machine and The Hobbit. They were both amazing. I tried lots of other books and I came to realise that even the ones that weren't my type of story could still be fun. I read horror, westerns, science fiction, adventure and several other types of books but no romance. Never romance.

My life throughout school was a mixture of borrowing books from the school library and saving up for the book club visits. I amassed quite a collection of my own books which I didn't need to hide. My parents had noticed I had become a bit of a book worm and didn't pay much attention to how many I had gathered. Once I was a little older, I convinced my mother to join the library so I could borrow more. I did prefer owning books, but I didn't always have the money to buy enough to feed my habit.

When I turned eighteen, I moved out of my parent's house into student accommodation. The one-bedroom apartment the university set me up in was tiny, but I asked my parents not to throw away any of my books, that I would be back for them and they agreed. At this point I began charity shop hunting. On a Saturday I would go into the city and go to every charity shop I could find. I would scour the book isles and always find lots of treasures. The prices were low so I could often pick up quite a few. Once read, I had to dump them in my old room at my parent's house. They had kept it as I had left it, only now there were piles of books everywhere. I could never bring myself to let go of a book once I owned it. It was different if it was from a library. I expected to take them back and for others to be able to read and enjoy them as well but when I bought one, it was mine for good.

I even kept all the books I had from those early days at school.

Throughout university I never really socialised with others. I was invited to plenty of parties and gatherings but there were just too many books I wanted to read and never enough time. No matter how quickly I read, I would find more books I wanted to read, and I would always buy more than I could get through. As time progressed, I had stacks of books at my parents that I hadn't started but knew I would read at some point. My old bedroom was beginning to look like a warehouse for books.

After I finished university, I had to give up my little room. It belonged to the university and they needed it for new students, so I moved back in with my parents. The problem was, there was almost no room in the bedroom other than the bed. I even had to move a lot of books from there. It didn't bother me, but my mum started to complain. I would spend every waking moment lying on my bed, reading several books at a time. I'd read a few chapters from one then start another, read a few chapters from that and start something else. Generally, when I got to about 5 books started, I would just go between them until I finished one or two then start some more.

After I had been back at my parents' for a few months, I was having dinner with them when my mother made what she thought to be a joke, but I thought was a great idea. She said that with all my books that I should open a book store. At first, I didn't like the idea of selling any of my books but then I began to think how much fun it would be sitting in a book store all day long, talking to others about books and as I sold some, I would have funds to go out and treasure hunt for more.

It took me a few months to speak to the right people about getting a small business loan then finding suitable premises, but with some hard work and a lot of time going from town to town buying stock, I was ready to open. Things went slow at first but as word spread, people came from all over to visit my little store. I think passionate readers enjoyed finding someone who was so well read to talk to, about their passion and get advice on other books they may like. I bought in more stock as I sold a lot of my early books quickly and I started to diversify. I bought limited edition books and signed or rare books. I have to say, it was the first time I had ever owned anything like that, but they were really special. When customers picked them up, I would get anxious. I really didn't want anyone to buy them, but I knew it was a shop I was running and if I didn't sell my stock, I would end up having to shut down.

A few months in and I was opening less hours every day. I just wanted people to come in and buy books I had already read or had more than one copy of and definitely not anything rare. The rare ones were often what drew the punters in, but a lot of the time they couldn't afford them and just wanted to look through them. I couldn't chance it though so instead of opening from nine to five, I opened from ten to four and I was closing longer for lunch every day. I used this time to walk around the store and smell the books, to touch them, just to be in their presence. I was in awe of them. How something so inanimate could make me feel so alive. I was finding that the more customers I had, the less time I had to read as they all wanted to talk to me, so I used the extra hours I had cut from store opening to plough through more books.

A couple of weeks later and I had changed opening hours from eleven to three and extended the lunch by a further hour. I had put a sign in the window with the hours, but people would still try the door and knock. I had blinds that pulled down and covered the whole window so no one could see in, but I could see their shadows. I was always there. I had set up a bed in the back of the shop but had taken to pulling the mattress through into the actual store, when I shut up for the night. I would lie there reading and gazing at the walls lined with books.

One night in particular as I lay on my mattress in the main store, I caught myself licking a page of a book and chewing on the corner. This seemed strange to me and I wondered if it was the first time I had done it. I wouldn't want to ruin any of my books and surely getting it wet was a quick way to do so. I let it slip from my mind and I began reading again. Five minutes later and I realised I was chewing on the corner again. I got up and placed the book on my desk. I went to a shelf where I had several copies of Richard Laymon's Beast House novel. I had been a big fan of Laymon for years, so I always picked up anything I had seen by him, which resulted in me

196

having four and five copies of some of his books. I sat in my comfy chair at the desk and I tore out the first page. I put it in my mouth, and I began to chew. It should have been bland and dry, but it wasn't. Various flavours filled my mouth as I chewed. It didn't even feel like paper. It felt like a medium rare piece of steak. I tore off another page and squashed it into my mouth as I swallowed the first. This one was light and tasted like strawberry cheesecake only was more flavoursome. I began asking myself questions. Was I mad, did I need help? Had books always been flavoured and people just didn't know. I tried another. Cheese and ham omelette that one tasted like.

After going through eleven or twelve different books that I had multiple copies of, I sat at my desk, feeling rather full. At some point in the night I must have passed out. When I awoke in the morning I was starving. Much hungrier than I had ever felt before. I wondered if this was because I knew I had such a feast at my fingertips. I began grabbing books from the shelves, tearing out a page and devouring them. There were pages that tasted of strawberry gummy bears, honey glazed ham, apple pie with cream, pancakes and syrup and too many more different taste sensations to mention. I ate until I could eat no more and once again, I fell asleep on my desk. There were people chapping on the door and window throughout the day, but I had grown used to that. I didn't open up but every few hours I would wake up and eat more.

Days passed and I didn't open the store. It now looked like a bomb had gone off. My once tidy store had books lying everywhere. Most with pages torn from them. I could hear people muttering outside. Maybe he's sold the store, or he always seemed strange to me or probably wasn't making enough money to keep it going. Everyone had a theory. Little did they know that I was the only one who wasn't insane. They should have all been at home, eating their books.

It was the next morning when I noticed that words had started to appear on my skin. Whole pages from different books were appearing as if I had them tattooed onto me, but I had never had a tattoo in my life. I didn't care. It was a small price to pay for knowing such a delicious secret. In the modern world, no one would notice. People would probably assume I paid quite a lot of money to have the pages tattooed onto me. Things were going just fine. My parents wouldn't miss me because I had been staying at the store anyway and they were happy to have some privacy and to have their spare room back after all those years.

Everything went fine for another week or two and then a problem arose. I started to become floppy. Just parts at a time but my left arm began to lose any solidity it had and would just wave about like a piece of paper caught in the wind. My left leg went next and then the fingers on my right hand. I've had to tape small pens to my fingers to keep them straight which was a feat in itself. It's taken me quite some time to type this out. I can still keep eating though. There are so many books lying everywhere I can literally just bite pages out of them. I can feel other parts of my body becoming floppier though. Almost all my skin is covered in paragraphs from books now. I fear the worst, I fear that I don't have long left before I myself am something book-like. It's been a good life though. Books have been good to me. In a way, they have been the only friend I've ever had. I just hope that someone looks after my books once I'm gone, the ones that I haven't partially eaten that is.

I better go now. I can feel my right arm starting to soften and I don't think I am capable of securing anything to it to keep it rigid. To whoever finds this note, if you find a book sitting on the chair at the desk, please don't eat it and please don't sell it on. Make sure that one gets to my mother and father.

The End

Printed in Poland
by Amazon Fulfillment
Poland Sp. z o.o., Wrocław